HANNAH

LOIS N. ERICKSON

REVIEW AND HERALD® PUBLISHING ASSOCIATION
HAGERSTOWN, MD 21740

The author assumes full responsibility for the accuracy of all facts and quotations as cited in this book.

Texts credited to NKJV are from The New King James Version. Copyright © 1979, 1980, 1982, Thomas Nelson, Inc., Publishers.

This book was
Edited by Gerald Wheeler
Designed by Patricia S. Wegh
Cover illustration by Barbara Kiwak
Typeset: 12/14 Palatino

PRINTED IN U.S.A.

99 98 97 96 95   10 9 8 7 6 5 4 3 2 1

R&H Cataloging Service

Erickson, Lois Nording, 1920-
    Hannah.

      I. Title.
        221.924

ISBN 0-8280-0867-1

Chapter 1

*H*annah sat on the side of a low hill, savoring a few moments of quiet before the evening chores. In the valley black goathair tents sprawled in a circle with herds of sheep, goats, donkeys, and oxen grazing nearby.

A sudden movement behind a juniper bush caught her attention, and she noticed the slight figure of her friend Peninnah. The girl scrambled up the hill and dropped down next to Hannah. Her gaze strayed to the eastern hills. "I wish I could stay up here forever."

"Has your father beaten you again?" Hannah asked gently.

Peninnah pushed back the sleeve of her robe and rubbed a dark bruise on her arm. "He hits me every day."

From below them an angry voice bellowed, "Daughter! Come milk these goats."

The girl jumped up, and Hannah could hear terror in her voice. "There he is now. I don't want to make him any angrier than he already is." She scurried down the rock-strewn hillside to the meadow. Hannah shuddered when she saw Peninnah's father grab her arm and slap her face. With a rough shove he pushed her toward the animals.

Trying to ease the pain she felt for her friend, Hannah hugged her brown woolen robe tighter around herself. Below the hill other girls walked toward the pasture, a reminder that it was milking time for her, too. She picked her way down through the juniper bushes to her family's tent and chose a goatskin bucket.

In the pasture she saw Peninnah crouched by the side of a black doe and brushing at tears that rolled down ugly red welts on her thin cheek. Hannah led one of her family's goats next to the girl and started to milk.

"I wish my father would arrange marriage for me so I could get away from him," Peninnah sobbed.

"But you're too young."

"No, I'm not. I'm 12 already. Just because you're 16 and not even promised doesn't mean I can't get married."

Finding no words to calm her friend's outburst, Hannah's thoughts shifted to her own problem. Why didn't her father find a husband for her? She knew the answer. Often enough he had told her he was increasing the size of his flocks until he acquired sufficient wealth to settle in some village or town. Then he would seek to arrange her marriage with a man from a city.

"Can't your father find a husband for you?" Peninnah persisted.

"You know he thinks I should marry a settler."

"That's what I want. A man who lives in a city with a thick wall around it where my father can't touch me."

Hannah pushed back her long dark-brown hair and held her hands to her flushed face. "That might be good for you, but if I ever have to live in a city, I'll feel trapped."

The girls carried the buckets of milk to their families' tents. Already shepherds were leading the herds into the center of the camp, there to watch over them during the night.

Hannah's mother, Abia, knelt by a limestone hearth. On it coals from her brush fire surrounded a clay pot of boiling lentils and barley. Using a basalt mortar and pestle, she pounded small, round coriander seeds to add to the thick soup. Years before, Hannah's father had first gathered stones to make this flat hearth, and each autumn the family returned to pitch their tent over it. It was their place, Hannah's favorite in all the territory of Ephraim.

As long as she could remember her family had camped here, a half-day journey from Shiloh. They arrived several weeks before Sukkot, the harvest Feast of Ingathering, so the animals could graze in the meadows and up along the hillsides. She savored the familiar sights and sounds . . . the wide, three-room tent with the fire on the hearth and smoke escaping out the open sides of the center room . . . the complaining sheep . . . the calls of the shepherds. Why would anyone want to leave all this to live in a city?

"Hannah." Her mother's voice broke into her thoughts. "Stop daydreaming and come stir the soup."

Kneeling by the small fire that glowed between the stones, Hannah used a wooden spoon to keep the family's supper from scorching. Wading through the flocks, her father and brother headed toward the tent. Hard work and the nomadic life kept Caleb and Jabal muscular and strong.

The men seated themselves on a rug near the open front of the tent's center room. While her mother poured milk into cups, Hannah placed unleavened bread and the pot of thick lentil and barley soup in front of her father and brother. They tore off pieces of bread and used them to scoop the soup into their mouths.

Abia handed a leather pouch to her daughter. "We need more water." Hannah slung the coarse flax ropes of the pouch over her shoulder and headed toward the well. It was an ancient watering place outside the ring of tents. As she walked across the rocky soil she noticed the sun had already sunk behind the hills, turning the western sky into streamers of gold. High above, the bright blue was beginning to deepen . . . the time of day when girls and women drew water from the well.

At the edge of a wide hole Hannah looked down. Limestone steps led to a clear pool at the bottom. Without hesitating she descended and quickly filled the goatskin pouch. Shaking off the moisture clinging to the outside, she settled it onto her shoulder. The heavy pouch slowed her ascent. Near the top she glanced up. Silhouetted against the bright western sky, a man waited. His white woolen headcovering hid the lower part of his face.

Abruptly Hannah stopped and held her breath. Why was he there? Men didn't come to the well in the evening. They drew water for the animals and poured it into chiseled stone troughs earlier in the day.

His voice grated into her thoughts. "Come up here."

Instantly she knew that voice. It was her cousin Medad. "Why are you here at the well?" she asked him.

"To talk to you."

After climbing the remaining few steps she stood facing him. "Why didn't you come to see me at my father's tent?"

"Huh," he snorted. "Your father! I talked to him this afternoon. Asked him why you weren't married. Thought we could make a bargain."

Hannah slid the water pouch to the ground. "A bargain for me?"

"He refused without even giving me a reason," Medad shouted. "Guess he thinks I'm not good enough to marry his daughter." Then he turned and strode toward the tents.

Raising the water pouch to her shoulder again, Hannah watched him walk away. *I wish I could marry someone from my own clan,* she brooded. *Maybe . . . maybe even Medad . . . if Father would only agree. But he wants me to marry a settler.* She shook her head and hurried back to her father's tent in time to see him put down his empty cup. "Make preparations, Abia," he said to his wife. "I have informed the men of our clan that tomorrow we travel to the Feast of Ingathering at Shiloh."

A surge of excitement flowed through Hannah. Shiloh and the Feast of Ingathering! Shiloh where the priests in the tabernacle guarded the ark of the covenant. As leader of the clan, her father had the right to decide when to take down the tents and journey on. Now he sat comfortably by the low fire while Hannah and her mother dipped their bread into the remaining soup. One of the black and gray striped cats that followed the clan patted its paw against Hannah's leg and begged for food. Glancing at her father and seeing that he was paying no attention, she placed a small portion of soup into her hand and offered it to the cat. The cats were descended from some that had been brought to the land years before by some Egyptian garrison or official. Hannah's people usually ignored the animals because of the fact that the Egyptians worshipped them as a symbol of some of their gods. But she always felt sorry for the creatures. The cat ate greedily and then licked his paws and cleaned his face.

Jabal returned to the flocks to take his turn with the other young men watching over the animals during the night. In the evening twilight Hannah rinsed the cups and cooking pot. Carefully she held the wick of a small, clay lamp into the fire. The wick, saturated with olive oil, gave a weak light, enough for her to see when she entered the women's end of the tent. Black and white woven rugs lay on top of the rocky soil in the small room. Thick white sheepskins and woolen blankets provided places for sleeping. Saddlebags, robes, her mother's loom, and straw baskets holding barley, wheat, garbanzos, and lentils left little space to walk around in the tent.

Removing her goatskin boots, Hannah settled back on the warm sheepskins. As she lay with her eyes open she thought about Shiloh and the Harvest Festival. This was the season when settlers picked pomegranates, dates, and figs. From their storage pits they brought out the first-fruits of wine and oil. Both nomads and settlers from many tribes traveled long distances to arrive at the Feast of Ingathering in these central mountains of Israel. There for seven days they feasted and danced and worshiped at the tabernacle to give thanks for the harvest. Eagerly she awaited the joyful celebration, the exciting processions, the captivating music of the Levites. Most people called Shiloh "The Place of Tranquillity" but Hannah always thought of it as "The Place of Merriment."

Still wearing her long brown robe, she pulled a blanket over her. Nights turned cold now that autumn had arrived.

Smiling in anticipation of the celebration, she clutched the blanket close to her chin. It gave a feeling of security even though she was alone in the room. During the nights that her brother watched the flocks, their mother slept in the men's end of the tent. A cat wandered in. With its head it lifted the edge of the blanket and snuggled under to sleep by Hannah's feet.

The following morning even before the sun's rays shone over the eastern hills, her father's voice rang out, "Make ready." Hannah and Abia gathered bowls and cooking pots, robes and sheepskins, water pouches and wineskins, and grain and fruit to load onto their donkeys. After removing the wooden tent poles and pulling up the oak stakes, they folded each separate room of the black goathair tent and placed them along with the rugs and the large cooking pot in the family's two-wheeled cart.

Abia was a solidly-built woman. Accustomed to the

hard nomadic life, she seldom complained about the heavy work, the long migrations, the heat of summer, or the cold rainy winter. Now she lifted her loom onto the loaded cart and sighed with relief that she had finished before her husband ordered the clan and their flocks to start out. Caleb brought two oxen and harnessed them to the cart. A cat leaped to the top of the load and settled down for the ride. Hannah's family ignored the Egyptian animal.

The cry "Forward!" resounded through the camp. Men and goats led the way with the sheep following, while women, children, laden donkeys, and the oxen pulling the carts trailed behind them. Guard donkeys without packs walked on either side of the sheep, ready to attack any wolf or jackal that threatened to snatch a lamb. Jabal and some of the young men protected the caravan's end.

Peninnah and Hannah walked side by side. "This year I'm old enough to dance with the women instead of just with the little girls," Peninnah announced. "I hope a man from a city will notice me."

Hannah frowned. "The dancing isn't to have a man notice you. It's to worship God and give thanks for the harvest."

"Not for me. I'm going to dance so a man will look at me." Peninnah paused a moment and then complained, "They already look at you, but just because you're bigger and prettier and your hair is darker than mine doesn't mean I can't have someone look at me." Her voice rose in excitement. "Maybe Benjaminites will hide in the vineyards, like they did once a long time ago, and grab some girls."

"You wouldn't want to go live with the tribe of Benjamin," Hannah exclaimed. "Don't forget you're an Ephraimite."

"My father would be glad to get rid of me."

Unable to think of a reply, Hannah made no answer. She gazed ahead to the front of their caravan where her father was turning the travelers onto the ancient highway that their ancestor Jacob and his wives Leah and Rachel had traveled long ago. It followed the crest of a ridge, and from here they could look down the eastern slope for their first glimpse of the hill city of Shiloh. The travelers gave joyful shouts. "The tabernacle! We can see the tabernacle on the top of the mount."

The light-colored limestone sanctuary that had replaced the ancient Tent of Meeting shone golden in the mid-day sunshine. Outside the thick city walls pilgrims had already arrived, and white smoke from their cooking fires rose in the still air. Beyond them, vineyards stretched toward the eastern mountains.

Caleb led the way down the hillside to flat land and then on to their traditional camping place. The caravan halted near a circle of crude shelters, close to other booths already occupied.

"I don't see why we can't put up our tents," Peninnah grumbled. "I don't like to sleep in a little booth without any sides on it."

"You know why we sleep in booths when we're at Shiloh. It's to remind us that our ancestors lived in the wilderness for 40 years, and we sleep like the harvesters do when they gather the grapes and figs and other crops."

"Ugh. I hate booths."

"But it's nice to see the stars," Hannah replied.

Peninnah wrinkled her nose and walked away.

As soon as the saddlebags rested on the ground, Jabal took the animals to a nearby hill. While the women gathered twigs and dry brush for their fires, men cut cedar boughs and myrtle branches to repair the shelters. Caleb examined his booth. Slender poles stuck in the ground supported additional poles across the top. He removed old branches from the top of the booth and replaced them with newly-cut cedar and myrtle.

Hannah stowed the saddlebags under the roof of branches. Her mother spread rugs, sheepskins, and blankets where the family would sleep. Later they heated a clay pan over the coals of their cooking fire and baked large rounds of flat wheat bread. They served it with warm goat milk, a simple supper before the next day's feasting.

In the darkness Hannah lay on her sheepskins and inhaled the pitchy smell of the cedar. Through the myrtle leaves she could see the first stars of the night. She gazed at them and watched until they grew brighter. Did her ancestors take time to appreciate the beauty of the heavens during those 40 years in the wilderness? Or were they too tired and discouraged? *How blessed I am to already live in the Promised Land,* she thought, *but I hope I never have to live in a city.*

Chapter 2

❧❦❧

*T*he soft call of a wood pigeon awoke Hannah and she glanced to the east. Rosy rays of light indicated that the sun would soon burst over the hills. She heard her father leave his sheepskins and rummage in the cart for a short-handled shovel. Her mother got up and took flint and pyrite to kindle a fire of dry grass and twigs.

Throwing off her blanket, Hannah stood up in the cold morning air. It was the day to prepare not only for the Sabbath but also for Sukkot and an exciting feast.

Caleb carried his shovel a short distance to a communal cooking area and with other men repaired the shallow, stone-lined pits for roasting lambs. They added stones where some had fallen during the winter rains and dug away the tall dry grass that had grown around the top edges.

Scrambling out of her own family's shelter, Peninnah dashed over to Hannah. "I want to dance right now," she said, swirling her robe about her.

"You know we have to wait until after sunset," Hannah reminded her although she, too, was eager for the festivities to begin. "Right now it's time to gather firewood." She reached into the cart and pulled out two nets made of coarse flax. The girls went some distance away to a stand of pines, and after gathering piles of dry branches that had fallen from the trees, they knelt to lift the filled nets.

"Ugh," Peninnah complained as she swung a bundle onto her back. "Heavy."

"We'll need more than these," Hannah commented. "Might as well take a good load each time."

Slowly they headed toward the cooking area. As they trudged into the encampment, a young man appeared around the end of a shelter. He was handsomely dressed in a brown and white striped robe and his dark hair and beard shone in the early morning sunshine. Hannah stopped abruptly, remembering him from the previous year's festival. She had often seen him talking with her brother near the communal cooking fires, and a few times she had noticed him glancing at her. What would she say if he spoke to her now?

"You look like you need help with those heavy loads," he observed with a smile.

Peninnah dropped hers to the ground. "Mine's too big."

"Let me carry it." He picked up the bundle and looked at Hannah. "Shall I take yours too?"

She shifted the branches higher on her back. Couldn't he see she wasn't just a thin little girl like Peninnah? Did her robe hide too well that she was fully developed and strong? "I can do it," she replied softly.

The man led the way, and Peninnah followed closely behind him. Hannah lingered a bit further back. Should she have accepted a stranger's offer of help? She hoped he didn't consider her rude for refusing it.

At the cooking area he dropped the bundle near a pit and spoke to Hannah. "Your father is Caleb, leader of this clan, isn't he?"

Proudly she raised her head and answered, "Yes, he is."

"I will have some business to discuss with him." The man headed back toward his booth.

Peninnah stared after him. "That's who I want to marry."

"But you don't know anything about him."

"I know he was nice enough to carry my wood." A wistful note crept into the girl's voice. "Do you think he lives in a city?"

"Of course. People who live in tents don't wear robes like that."

Along with the other women and girls, Hannah and Peninnah brought back more bundles of branches. Then they gathered dry grass and twigs to start fires in the pits, adding pine and oak from time to time until the pits glowed with hot coals.

"Make ready," the leaders of nomadic clans and the chieftains of the settlers shouted. "Make ready for the Sabbath Eve sacrifice." Soon they led lambs toward Shiloh's narrow gate and filed onto the stone-paved street to proceed toward the tabernacle. The wide street branched, one way leading to the marketplace, the other becoming a wide stairway that rose gradually to the top of the hill. Boots and sandals slapped against the stone, and lambs' hooves beat an irregular rhythm. Women and children followed the men up the stairway and through a gate in a thick wall, and then the tabernacle courtyard spread before the worshipers.

A dignified man wearing a rich garment of gold, scarlet, blue, and purple walked out of the tabernacle. Two young men in similar dress and a group of white-robed priests followed him. The man raised his right hand. "I, your high priest Eli, my sons Hophni and Phinehas, and the chief priests welcome you to Sukkot, the Feast of Ingathering. Take your sacrifices to the altar."

The men circled the large courtyard altar. Made of uncut limestone blocks, it stood higher than a man's waist. A hot fire burned on the soil and clay that filled a cavity in the center.

Eli's voice rang out over the assembled people. "Place your hands on the heads of your animals and dedicate them to God." A heavily-built man, he had a commanding manner. The worshipers did as he asked. "We dedicate these animals and give thanks that God has forgiven our sins."

"Go in peace," Eli declared.

The men returned with the sheep to the pasture and then brought them to the cooking area, butchered, ready to roast or boil. Three cats followed Hannah's father and brother. Jabal handed a fresh sheepskin to his mother, and she spread it on the ground with the wool side down. Immediately the half-wild cats pounced on it. With their rough tongues they scraped the moisture and bits of flesh off the sheepskin until it was well cleansed.

Caleb and Jabal skewered a long iron rod through their lamb and then laid it over the top of a pit. Hot coals glowed and a smoky odor of roasting meat spread through the air. Abia picked up her sheepskin and carried it to their shelter. There she washed it with cold, heavily-salted water. Using a flax rope she tied it to the outside of the wooden cart, stretching it to dry. That accomplished, she and Hannah turned their attention to the task of preparing a two-day supply of bread, and to rotate the meat when necessary to cook it evenly on all sides. Vendors laid out their wares near the pits, and women came to buy food for the Sabbath. Abia traded part of a woolen fleece for three baskets of pomegranates, dates, figs and pistachio nuts, and enough new wine to fill two pouches. Men, too, made their preparations, gathering palm, myrtle, and willow branches for the next morning's procession.

17

During the afternoon Hannah glanced often toward the southern sky to check the progress of the sun . . . such a long wait until sundown when the festivities would begin. At last all the men congregated by the pits. They too watched the sun as it sank slowly behind the western hills. As the final bright spot disappeared a great shout went up. "Let the Feast of Ingathering begin."

Men removed the roasted lambs from the fires and laid them on beds of palm leaves. With sharp flint knives they cut the right leg and breast from each lamb and placed these pieces into clay pans. Other pans held uncooked fat.

Then, as Hannah watched the men march to the city gate, Peninnah came to stand beside her. "Why don't they walk faster? My father said I can't eat till he comes back."

"I want to eat too," Hannah confessed, "but you know we have to wait while they give meat to the priests and burn fat on the altar." The girls sat down on a rug and gazed toward the tabernacle. The courtyard wall hid the assembled men and the altar, but soon thick smoke rose toward the sky. Excitedly Hannah pointed to it. "Look! Smoke from the burning fat is rising straight up to the sky. God is accepting the sacrifice."

"I'm hungry," Peninnah grumbled.

When Caleb and Jabal returned to the camp, Abia and Hannah laid out bowls and cups. Caleb's flint knife cut into the remainder of the lamb. He served Jabal first and then Abia and Hannah, dropping meat into their bowls and handing bread to them. Lifting a wineskin to his lips he drank from its spout before handing it to his son, wife, and daughter.

The people of Hannah's clan seated themselves on the grass, laughing, talking, eating, drinking. A short distance behind Caleb's back, Jabal and his cousin Medad sat together. Medad looked over at Hannah and a broad smile indicated his pleasure at eating with her family even though her father was unaware of it. A fleeting thought tantalized her. *Maybe Father will reconsider . . .*

As the feasting drew to a close, the young unmarried men wandered away from their families and sought out eligible unmarried girls to visit. Under the watchful eyes of the girls' parents they sat as close as allowed to the chosen young women. Hannah yearned for Medad to sit with her, but she suspected that her father would not allow him nor any other nomad to choose her.

In the lingering twilight the evening began to grow cold. As she placed a shawl around her shoulders, she looked up to see the young man who had offered to carry the firewood walking toward her family. He glanced in her direction and then stopped in front of Caleb. Hannah looked down at the grass and worried to herself, *I hope he hasn't come to complain because I was impolite.*

"I'm here to ask if I might speak with you some day during this festival," he said to her father.

"I conduct no business, neither buying nor selling, until after the end of the third day," Caleb declared, indicating that he intended to control any bargaining that might take place.

The man paused briefly before replying, "I'm willing to wait until after the end of the third day."

Caleb raised his hand. "As leader of my clan and head of my family, I grant permission for you to speak with me at that time."

"Then I will tell you my name. I am Elkanah son of Jeroham. I am a Levite from the town of Ramah."

"I am Caleb, an Ephraimite who wanders the land with his sheep and goats."

Elkanah bowed his head. "After the third day's feast,

I will come."

"I pray you," Caleb replied, offering the customary hospitality, "feast with me that day at sundown."

"You are most generous. I will feast with you." He backed away and then strode toward a well-dressed woman who stood by a booth observing him.

Fascinated, Hannah watched him go. He walked easily, strong as a nomad, yet with an added assurance that she had never noticed in any other man.

"Who is he?" Peninnah's eager whisper echoed in her ear.

"Oh, I didn't see you come."

The younger girl drew down the corners of her mouth. "Too busy admiring the handsome man?"

"No," Hannah protested, "I was just watching him leave." She stood up and tried to walk away but Peninnah followed her.

"Did you find out his name?"

"He told my father his name is Elkanah."

"What city is he from?"

"From Ramah."

"Ramah! It's on a high hill with a big wall around it. If I dance in front of that man, maybe he'll want to marry me." Peninnah circled with her hands held high but stopped to ask, "Why was he talking with your father?"

"I'm not sure. Maybe he wants to buy some sheep. Oh, look! My father is lighting a torch. It's time to go to the tabernacle."

The younger girl twisted her mouth into a pout. "I wish we could dance in the vineyards like the women used to. Now, just because those Benjaminites grabbed girls in the vineyards a long time ago, our fathers are too strict."

Lights of numerous torches appeared, and the percussion of polished olivewood sticks hitting bronze cymbals vibrated in the still evening air. The Levites led the way into the city and up to the tabernacle. From all the tribes of Israel each leader of clan or city preceded his people into the courtyard. The rectangular tabernacle with its two stately doorposts rested like a blessing in front of them. The beauty of the structure caused Hannah to draw in a deep, reverent breath.

Now the Levites stepped onto the tabernacle porch and along with white-robed priests continued the music, adding their deep voices in song. "Praise to God on high. Praise to the Almighty. Praise. Praise. Praise." While the men continued to hold their torches high, young unmarried women and girls advanced to the large courtyard altar. "Thank You, God of our ancestors," Hannah whispered her prayer. "Praise to You for guiding our lives." In graceful rhythm she paced forward.

The women and girls circled the altar with leisurely steps . . . swaying gently . . . holding their hands, palms upward, high above their heads. As they danced toward the tabernacle, the flickering light from the men's torches revealed the singing Levites. One of them wore a brown and white robe.

Peninnah edged close to Hannah as they danced around the altar. "Do you see him?" she asked in a low voice. "He's watching me."

Chapter 3

❦

*T*hey always face toward the courtyard," Hannah tried to calm the excited girl. "But that doesn't mean they're looking at anyone in particular." She glanced toward the musicians and missed a step in the dance. It was true—Elkanah *was* staring directly at her and Peninnah.

The girl's lower lip pouted. "You don't care anything about me. No one does." She circled away.

Hannah retreated to the altar and lifted her hands and heart in prayer. "Lord, some day please let Peninnah know that I do care about her," she whispered.

Above the tops of oak trees the full harvest moon began to rise. An orange ball in the dark sky, it cast its light onto the festive worshipers in the courtyard. Finally the voices of the singers faded and music of the cymbals ceased. Even though she was reluctant to leave the beauty of the tabernacle, Hannah followed her father and mother through the dark city streets and out to their shelter. As she lay on her sheepskins, she noticed the flames from the surrounding campfires and heard laughter echoing from booths. Some of the young men were already drinking too much new wine.

In the morning the clang of cymbals awoke her as the Levites marched through the camp to call the people for worship. Her father's bed was empty, and she turned over to see him selecting palm, willow, and myrtle branches from those he had saved in a pile. Her mother chose pomegranates, figs, and bread from baskets. The high-pitched notes of flutes joined the rhythm of the cymbals.

Hannah draped a shawl over her long brown hair and then followed her father, mother, and brother toward the city gate where the rest of the pilgrims were gathering. She watched the crowd until she caught sight of the young man from Ramah. He was waiting with several other Levites to lead the people to the tabernacle. Quickly she glanced down at the pomegranates in her basket, hoping he hadn't seen her searching for a glimpse of him.

Men carried the intertwined branches while the women and children brought fruit and bread. The worshipers entered the courtyard and marched around the altar, singing "Give to God glory and praise." Holding baskets in their hands, Eli and the priests came out of the tabernacle and accepted the food.

Later, back at the booth, the family relaxed. It was the Sabbath, a holy time of freedom from labor. They had prepared well the day before . . . gathered wood for the fire, baked bread, bought fruit and nuts. Now they could enjoy a day of rest.

With a contented groan, Caleb lay down on his sheepskins for a morning nap. Medad sauntered past and motioned for Hannah to follow him toward the pasture. Knowing her father would not approve, she shook her head. Scowling at the sleeping man, he turned away.

For Hannah and Peninnah the day passed slowly until at last the sun sank behind the hills. The girls milked their goats, and the families feasted on warm milk, pomegranates, dates, pistachio nuts, and bread until time to proceed to the tabernacle. Abia handed small baskets of fruit and bread to her husband and son.

At the entrance to the courtyard Peninnah whispered

to Hannah. "Look at the robes the women from Shiloh are wearing tonight."

Hannah, too, had noticed how the local young women were dressed. "I guess they have enough wealth to buy fine Egyptian linen." She smoothed the side of her coarse linen robe. "I like this natural color better."

"Some day I'm going to have robes of fine linen," Peninnah insisted. "Then I'll never wear coarse linen again."

The soaring notes of flutes and the men's rich singing drew the worshipers into the courtyard. Holding their torches high, the men paced forward with food for the priests. Suddenly Eli's son Hophni grabbed several rounds of bread out of Jabal's basket before he could offer it. Hannah gasped. She had heard that Hophni and Phinehas were greedy but never before had seen them in action.

Now it was time to worship at the altar. Hannah raised her hands in prayerful adoration and bowed before the holy place. "Praise to the Eternal One," sang the Levites. As Hannah circled the altar, she glanced toward the singers and her heart skipped. Elkanah was scanning the dancers as if searching for someone. Was he hoping to see Peninnah? She continued her worship but was careful not to look at the musicians.

The following morning the men marched around the altar again, offering fruit and bread, and at sundown the people repeated the evening worship as they would each day of the festival. The morning of the third day Caleb instructed his wife and daughter, "Prepare well for our guest. He's a settler and, no doubt, accustomed to fine food."

"I'll grind the wheat," Hannah offered. She dropped handfuls of grain into a large granite mortar and, with a heavy granite pestle, pounded the wheat into flour. Her mother kindled fire in a ring of stones near their booth.

Late that afternoon Caleb returned from the pasture to check on the preparations. Abia smiled in satisfaction. "We've baked bread, and the stew is nearly ready." She rubbed cumin between the palms of her hands and let the bruised seeds fall into the garbanzo and onion stew.

"I made goat cheese," Hannah reported. She had boiled curdled milk for half the day, adding honey and a small amount of flour to prepare the sweet, brown cheese.

"What else?" asked her father. "I want to make a good impression on any settler who comes to me."

Abia pointed to a basket. "We have good dates, figs, and pistachio nuts." After nodding his approval, Caleb returned to care for his flocks.

"Your father is acting strangely." Abia's voice rose to a nervous pitch. "I've never seen him so concerned about a guest."

Sudden uncertainty clutched at Hannah. "I wonder why that man Elkanah wants to talk to Father."

Shaking her head, her mother stirred the stew. "Your father needs more silver and gold before we can settle. He's hoping the man wants to buy some sheep."

A few clouds gathered on the horizon and the sun sank behind them. A chilling breeze blew from the west. Jabal and Caleb arrived from the pasture and sat close to the fire. Seated in the booth Hannah combed her hair and placed a brown woolen shawl around her shoulders. She looked in the direction of Elkanah's shelter, but drew back when she saw him walking toward her father.

Caleb stood and stepped forward. "Welcome to my fire." He motioned to a rug and invited his guest to sit down. Hannah peeked out of the booth at the man's back. He sat straight and formal opposite her father and brother. "Come, daughter, and serve our guest," Caleb called.

Hannah brought salt in a clay cup and bread on a linen cloth. She set them before her father. He broke a flat round of bread into three parts and gave one to Elkanah. "In peace I offer this bread."

The young man dipped his bread into the salt. "In peace I accept your bread." Caleb and Jabal added salt to their bread and ate with him.

Abia removed the cooking pot from the fire and set the steaming stew in front of the men. As Hannah handed more bread to the guest, her fingers accidentally touched his. In her confusion she nearly dropped the bread. He smiled at her but said nothing. Abia carried a wineskin to her husband, and Hannah placed fruit and cheese on linen cloths. Then the women retreated to the booth.

By the time the three men finished their leisurely meal, the sky held only a trace of orange in the west. "You asked to speak with me after the third day," Caleb prompted the young Levite.

Elkanah gave the polite reply. "You are kind to allow me the honor."

The older man spoke the traditional words for conducting business. "If you wish any of my property, please state your needs."

"I have but one request." Elkanah hesitated a moment. In the booth the women leaned forward to hear what he would ask. "I am a Levite, a descendant from Levi's son Kohath," they heard him say. "During the leadership of Moses, my family was assigned as priests, scribes, and teachers to the tribe of Ephraim. Now I need a son to carry on our traditions. The time has come for me to marry . . . and I wish to have your daughter for my wife."

Hannah sank to the floor of the booth. Her marriage to a settler—this was what her father craved, and she could make it possible, but she would have to live behind walls. Abia drew in a sharp breath. "I thought he wanted to buy sheep."

Caleb gazed into the fire before answering. "My daughter? I have only one, and she is very dear to me. How would you provide for her?"

"I am a teacher as my father was before me," Elkanah replied with confidence. "I teach young boys to read and write, and I instruct them in how to worship God."

Caleb allowed silence to flow between them before asking, "What can you offer?"

"What do you consider a fair exchange for this arrangement?"

With a shrug of his shoulders Caleb commented, "I do not want to put you to any trouble, but for some time I have planned to settle. My clan is too small to build its own city. We will have to move, a few at a time, into existing settlements. A city on a hill would be my choice."

The young man spoke slowly. "My father is no longer living, and my brothers also have died. My house has unused space." He stroked his beard as if in deep contemplation. "I can give you two chambers in my home."

Now Caleb placed his hand on his beard. "And I can provide lambs for the wedding feast."

With a catch in her breath Hannah whispered to her mother, "I wonder what it's like to live in a house."

"Hush. They're talking again."

"This is my pledge," Caleb declared. "I promise my daughter to you along with enough lambs for the wedding feast."

Elkanah stood. "I promise to provide two rooms for you in my house."

Caleb rose to face him. "Before sundown on the seventh day of this feast I will announce your betrothal."

The young man looked toward the booth. "Come, Hannah," her father ordered. "Come and greet the man to whom you're promised." She could hear the satisfied tone in his voice.

Slowly she advanced toward the fire. Elkanah stepped forward to meet her. He took hold of her hand and held it in his large, warm one. Tingles ran along her arm, and she suddenly found that she needed to breathe deeply. Then she looked up into his dark eyes. Moonlight shone on his face, and she could see his smile. He could write and read and sing. She was only a nomad who could milk a goat. Why would he want her? What could she offer such a man?

"A year from now I will take you for my wife." He waited for some reaction from her.

"I . . . I hope," she stammered, "to give you many sons to carry on your traditions." His smile became broader, and he reached for her other hand. They stood for a moment, gazing into each other's eyes. Then he spoke briefly to her father and brother before returning to his booth.

Chapter 4

❧❧❧

*I*n the morning Hannah picked up her wood-gathering net and headed toward the trees. The sound of running footsteps caused her to look around. As Peninnah caught up with her, she demanded, "Why was that man eating at your fire last night?"

Reluctant to give the reason, Hannah answered, "My father invited him."

"Did he want to buy some sheep?"

"No."

"Why won't you tell me anything?"

Closing her eyes to blot out the frown on the girl's face, Hannah said, "He asked for me, and my father promised."

Horrified, Peninnah stepped back. "Promised! You're promised to the man I want to marry? And you always say you're my friend."

"I am your friend," Hannah insisted, "but my father gave his word. You know we never have any choice."

Sobbing, Peninnah ran toward the juniper bushes on the hillside.

Hannah longed to comfort her friend yet hesitated to do so. Maybe that would only cause more resentment in the girl. As she walked toward the grove of pines, her thoughts turned to the night before and the thrill of Elkanah's hand on hers, his deep voice saying, "I will take you for my wife." She sighed. If only he were a nomad . . . but then . . . her father wouldn't have promised her to a wanderer.

With the net full of firewood she pulled the heavy load onto her back. Straightening up, she saw Elkanah walking toward her. "This time may I carry your load?" he asked with his pleasant smile.

She smiled in return. "You may." He lifted it from her back and onto his. Standing so close, she felt a sudden desire to place her hand in his. No, she mustn't. What would he think of such a bold action?

At her booth he dropped the wood near the fire ring. "I have asked permission from your father to walk with you each day before sundown." He touched her shoulder and then left to summon the men for worship. Hannah watched him go, once again admiring his self-assurance. Pensively she placed her hand on the spot he had touched.

Before sundown he returned and the well-dressed woman Hannah had noticed accompanied him. She wore a cream-colored robe with neatly-stitched embroidery of yellow and blue at the neck. "My mother Taphath," he announced, introducing her to Caleb and Abia and then to Hannah.

Taphath embraced her future daughter-in-law and kissed her on both cheeks. "At last I'll have grandsons! You're a lovely young woman, and we're happy to share our home with you."

How many rooms does it have? Hannah wondered silently. *Where will I bake bread?*

"Our house is large," Taphath babbled on. "Room for many children. Too bad betrothal time lasts for a year. I wish you could come with us at the end of this festival."

Overwhelmed by the woman's enthusiasm, Hannah managed only a polite reply. "You're very kind."

"Come sit with me," Abia invited Elkanah's mother. The two women retired to the booth. Caleb settled down by the fire with his back to the young couple. Suddenly aware that now she had the right to walk with this man standing near her, Hannah gazed at the distant hills. When he took her hand, she turned toward him. His broad smile sent a flutter through her breast.

They walked toward the vineyards. His voice broke through her thoughts. "I saw you last year at this festival," he was saying.

"I remember you talked with my brother," she admitted.

"I wish I had spoken with your father at that time." He shook his head. "Now I have to wait another year before I can take you into my house."

Silent questions thrust themselves at Hannah. *Will I feel lonely next year when my clan migrates south without me? I'll never forget the evenings by the fire and Mother repeating stories of our ancestors . . . how Joshua, an Ephraimite, charged his tribe to invade the land and claim this territory. How much colder is winter in Ramah than in the southern part of Ephraim? Where will I gather wood? Is the house dark and gloomy?*

Elkanah's voice again broke into her thoughts. "You're very quiet."

"I've never lived in a house," she suddenly said, then stopped and looked down at her feet.

He took both of her hands in his. "I think you'll like it."

They strolled near the pasture. "I own a few sheep and goats," he said. "Of course, I hire a shepherd to take them to pasture each day."

"I can help with the milking," Hannah suggested.

"That isn't necessary. Our maidservants do the milking. We have two and a manservant."

And what are my responsibilities? Hannah asked herself. *Just produce sons?*

Each evening before sundown Elkanah appeared at her father's fire, and she walked with him. They admired the rise of a hill, the height of a cypress, the flight of an eagle. It had never occurred to Hannah that a city dweller could appreciate the beauty of God's creation.

On the sixth day Caleb ordered some boys to carry news to the clan. Scurrying among the people, they yelled, "Our leader commands every man, woman, and child to gather in front of his booth before sundown." Hannah went early to draw water for washing her face and hands. Then, dressed in her coarse linen robe and brown woolen shawl, she sat in the booth with her mother and waited for Elkanah to arrive.

Before sundown the clan gathered around Hannah's father's booth. When she heard his voice ring out, she closed her eyes and listened to him declare, "I, your leader, have summoned you to witness my decree. I pronounce that from this moment my daughter Hannah is betrothed to a Levite from Ramah, Elkanah son of Jeroham. This betrothal shall last for one year and the marriage feast will take place after the next harvest festival."

"Bring out the maiden," the people shouted.

When she opened her eyes, Hannah noticed tears on her mother's cheeks and found that she needed to blink away her own moisture. Without speaking they embraced briefly before leaving the booth to face the members of the clan. Caleb stood proudly before the people with Elkanah on his right. At the sight of him, Hannah's heart beat rapidly. She stopped for a moment to take a deep breath before she advanced to stand to the left of her father. He placed her hand in Elkanah's and then held his own on top of theirs.

Now greater shouts went up. "We're witnesses. We witness this betrothal."

Hannah looked out at the clan. Near the back she saw the scowling face of her cousin Medad. Next to him Peninnah bowed her head and placed her hands over her eyes.

Caleb raised his hand and proclaimed, "Take your offerings and worship to the tabernacle, and then let the evening feasting commence."

Elkanah's voice broke forth in song. "Praise to our God. Praise. Praise. Praise to the Almighty." The beauty of the sacred words sent a shiver through Hannah. When he turned toward her, she could see a deep longing in his eyes. Forgetting for the moment her dread of living in a city, she smiled back at him.

While the men carried fruit and bread to the priests, Elkanah's mother lingered to talk to Hannah. "I will fashion your wedding gown of fine Egyptian linen," she announced. "It's the only appropriate fabric for the bride of a Levite who lives in Ramah. I have chosen purple, and I'll weave a white shawl of goat's wool."

"You're very kind," Hannah replied respectfully. She looked down at her coarse linen robe and tried to envision herself in a gown of fine purple linen. Would Elkanah prefer her in fine linen rather than coarse linen and brown wool?

The men returned and the feasting began. The betrothed couple sat together near the fire's warmth. Caleb broke bread and gave a portion to his future son-in-law. Elkanah divided the piece and offered half of it to Hannah. Amazed at his generosity, she ate her bread and fruit in silence while she listened to her mother and Taphath discuss wedding plans. Her father and Elkanah spoke of sheep and goats. Then they lowered their voices, and the only words she could hear were "Philistines in Judah."

The sound of cymbals announced that it was time to

worship. Levites began their chant, and Elkanah joined them in a song of praise. As she danced in front of the altar, Hannah remembered the festival's first night when Peninnah thought Elkanah was watching her. Now the girl failed to appear at the worship and the man in the brown and white robe watched only Hannah.

In the morning a cool wind blew clouds from the west. Impatient to pack and head south, Caleb glared at the gloomy sky. Hannah hurried to help her mother load the cart and secure the packs on the donkeys while her father and brother led the flocks from the pasture. She glanced often in the direction of Elkanah's booth, wondering if he would speak with her again before the caravan started out. She could see his mother packing baskets and saddle bags. Then he appeared leading a donkey. Leaving it near his belongings, he came to Hannah and placed his hand gently on her arm. "Until next year," he whispered. As she watched him walk away, an empty feeling seized her.

Caleb and Jabal brought the oxen and hitched them to the cart. In the gray morning light the cry "Forward" resounded, and the clan headed south. A mist descended and then a steady rain fell on the travelers. Hannah shook her woven goathair cloak to remove some of the water. Once she glanced back at Shiloh, but the city and tabernacle were barely visible in the clouds.

By late afternoon the rain ceased and a few patches of blue appeared among the gray and white clouds. The weary travelers put up their tents in a meadow where they would take their Sabbath rest. Hannah gazed westward and thought about the hill city of Ramah, a day's journey away. In years past she and her mother had entered there more than once to buy grain and lentils, but had visited only shops on the lower terrace. Never had she ventured up to the higher levels where the homes clung to the sides of the hill. *On which terrace is the house where I will live?* she wondered.

Three more days of travel brought the nomads close to the territory of Dan. There they would winter, occasionally moving the flocks to find new pasture along the border. Many days during that season the rains beat down upon the earth, but the people didn't complain. They gave thanks for the moisture that promised good summer grazing in the meadows. Their heavy cloaks protected them, and the fibers in the goathair tents expanded when wet until the dwellings let in no water.

One afternoon when the clouds had rolled away, Hannah wandered into the pasture to enjoy a solitary stroll. Near a large rock she spotted a blue hyacinth—the first sign of spring. She knelt to inhale the flower's exotic fragrance. One of her father's guard donkeys ambled over to her and rested its head on her shoulder, asking for affection. With firm strokes she rubbed its neck. A pensive longing to hold onto this moment and this way of life swept over her.

Suddenly the donkey raised its head and trotted closer to the flock. Beyond him a man stumbled across the clearing. "Help me," he called. Fear of the stranger clutched at Hannah until she saw Jabal and two other shepherds racing her way. They panted to a stop just as the man fell to the ground. "Have mercy on me," he pleaded.

"Arise, stranger. We are peaceful men," Jabal assured him. "We wish you no harm."

With great effort he stood up. "I need food and a place to sleep this night."

"Who are you and why are you wandering alone in the territory of Ephraim?" one of the shepherds asked.

"I'm from Judah. A few days ago I pastured my flock

too close to the Philistines who occupy our coastal lands. They forced me to carry a heavy pack and travel with them as they pushed farther into the territory of Dan. Yesterday I escaped and fled until I saw your flocks."

"Come," Jabal ordered. "We must take this news to my father." They walked together toward the edge of the clearing where the clan's tents waited under a grove of terebinth oak trees.

Philistines in Dan! The very thought sent a chill through Hannah. They had already invaded and occupied the coast of Judah, but now these Sea People were encroaching on the coast land of Dan. Although Ephraim didn't border on the great western sea, Hannah had heard her father mention many times that an easy two-days' march could bring invading Philistines into their own territory.

Chapter 5

❦

*W*hile they served lentils and bread to Caleb and the traveler, Hannah and Abia listened to his frightening tale. "When we see large ships with images of bird's heads on either end, we know that more Sea People will invade our land," he said. "They constantly unload their chariots and wagons, their women and little ones."

"Why don't your men go out to fight these invaders?" Caleb demanded.

"We are no match," the man replied sadly. "Their spears are longer than ours. Whenever we've tried to defend our land, we've always been defeated. Now the sight of their tall, feathered headdresses strikes us with dread."

That night the stranger slept by the fire in the center room of Caleb's tent. Early in the morning he accepted Abia's bread to carry with him on his journey back to his own land.

"Make ready to leave this valley," Caleb directed his people. "We will travel eastward over the mountains to the River Jordan—beyond the range of Philistine raiding parties." The women hurried to pack, and the clan soon headed northeast toward a well-known pass in the mountain range. Three days later they left the pass behind them and camped by a small stream that flowed toward the river. Through that winter and the following summer they pastured their flocks in the Jordan Valley.

Flax grew plentifully in the moist soil along the Jordan. Together with the other women and girls of her clan Hannah went out to pull the mature plants. Near the water's edge she saw Peninnah bending down to pull a stalk. Although she worried about how the girl would react, she said, "I wish we could be friends again."

When Peninnah straightened up, Hannah saw tears in her eyes. Without a word the girl walked away. For a moment Hannah stared at her, then resumed harvesting the flax. She carried her bundle of stalks to the side of her father's tent. When she returned for more, Peninnah was nowhere in sight.

Hannah and her mother placed the flax in nets and submerged them in the river, securing the nets with ropes tied to willows along the bank. Several days of soaking loosened the strands of fiber enough so the women could pound the stalks with heavy wooden mallets to free them.

After combing to draw out the strong, thin strands, they had the pale yellow flax ready for spinning. It was a task that Hannah and Peninnah had always enjoyed together. They would hold the distaff high in their left hands while they pulled and twisted the long, damp fibers onto the spindle in their right hands. At the same time they would chat and confide and tell each other their secret hopes. Now Peninnah stayed in her father's tent while she spun the flax strands into linen yarn.

When the leaves started to turn brown and fall to the ground, Caleb began to scan the sky each day. One cool morning a sign appeared . . . the first of the wood pigeons flying south. "Make ready," he announced. "Tomorrow we head toward the northern pass to cross over the mountains on our way to Shiloh."

The harvest festival! Confused thoughts raced

through Hannah's mind . . . a desire to worship at the tabernacle . . . a sadness that she would soon leave her clan . . . a pensive longing to see Elkanah. Fourteen days later Caleb led his people toward the booths outside the holy city. As she walked along, Hannah glanced tensely from side to side. Had the people from Ramah already arrived? After a year apart, was Elkanah still as eager to see her as she was him?

When her father halted the caravan, Hannah lifted the heavy cooking pot from the cart and knelt to place it in the booth. Behind her a deep voice spoke softly. "Hannah." When she stood, Elkanah's arms enclosed her, and she rested her head against his strong shoulder. "It was a long year without you," he whispered into her ear.

Caleb's hearty greeting intruded into their embrace. "Welcome, future son-in-law. My daughter will build a fire so we can sit in comfort."

"You're very kind, but first I must repair my booth. Later I'll return to accept your hospitality."

Still savoring the warmth of his arms around her, Hannah watched him walk away. Then she turned her attention to removing the packs from the donkeys. As she lifted the last one, Elkanah's mother hurried toward her, a smile spread across her face. "I've made your wedding gown, and it's beautiful, full and flowing, long enough to cover sandals, not just to the top of boots. It's a lovely shade of purple, and I embroidered golden threads at the neckline."

Hannah looked down at her brown robe and dusty boots. She tried to envision herself in a purple and golden gown. At least when she became a settler and needed to think of her nomad days she would be able to go to her mother's room, and they could talk about long treks through the forests and sleeping in a tent. "Thank you for preparing my gown." She hoped her answer to Taphath sounded gracious.

Each evening during the week of the harvest festival, Elkanah came to sit by the fire. So close in time to the wedding it was not proper for the betrothed couple to walk by themselves. While merrymakers drank new wine, while Levites sang, while men carried sacrifices to the priests, Hannah mused about this her last festival as a maiden. Yet when she danced with the unmarried women, she basked in the admiring gaze of the man from Ramah.

On the festival's final night Elkanah and his mother took the evening meal with Caleb's family. They drew close to the fire for warmth against a cool western breeze. Caleb laid down the bread he was eating and spoke to Elkanah. "In preparation for settling in Ramah, I have talked to Jabal about assuming leadership of the clan." He paused, staring absently into the fire. "But my son is young with no experience as a leader . . . and now the Philistines. I have spoken with leaders from Judah and Dan. They tell me that more and more Sea People are leaving their island home and invading Israel to settle into our land." His voice rose. "Where will they advance next? I cannot leave my people at this time. I must continue to lead them."

Hannah's head bent forward and her thoughts whirled. *Father is the one who wants to live in town, and I thought I was helping him. If the Philistines invade Ephraim, will the clan be able to find refuge on the east side of the mountains? I've heard others insist that the safest place is in a walled city like Ramah, but even there if an enemy surrounds it, how can anyone escape?*

"I understand your concern for your people," Elkanah replied, "and I respect your judgment." He paused briefly before adding, "Since you will not use the rooms in my house, I will provide the traditional bride price."

Caleb nodded in agreement. "So be it."

In the morning Hannah helped her mother pack the cart. Frost crunched under their boots, and they paused to blow warm breath on their cold fingers. "I wanted to settle near you," Abia said firmly, "but now your father refuses even though Jabal is perfectly capable of leading the clan."

Hannah gazed toward the hills, and her voice was only a whisper. "I wish you could live in Ramah."

In the dim light Elkanah appeared with his mother and their loaded donkey. He stopped next to Hannah. "Since I carry no tent, my mother and I must reach an inn before evening." For a moment he gazed into her eyes, then turned to start the journey toward his home.

A short while later Caleb shouted, "Forward!" and the people took their places in the caravan. That day they marched up to the highway and then west and south through the hill country. Their steady progress brought them halfway to Ramah before sundown. The following day they resumed their trek, and by late afternoon pitched their tents at a camping place reserved for travelers where they would not encroach on the cultivated fields and pasture that surrounded Ramah.

Hannah stood outside the tent and observed the houses on the terraced hill clearly visible above the double walls encircling the city. "This shall be my home," she whispered to herself. "So new and strange except . . . except I'll be there with him."

The afternoon of the next day Hannah drew water from the well near their camp and carried it to the tent for bathing. Then seated on her sheepskins, she waited. Familiar sounds came through the tent walls . . . the soft calls of wood pigeons flying south, the crackle of the fire in the center room. When the sun began to sink behind the hills, she lit the wick in a clay lamp. Abia entered the tent. "I see your young man's mother walking this way, and a maidservant with her is carrying a basket."

Hannah rubbed her hand across her brown robe. "I guess she's bringing the purple gown." She stood and opened the tent flap to welcome her future mother-in-law.

Taphath hurried in, followed by the young maidservant. "I've brought the gown." She took the basket from the maid and pulled out a fine linen garment. Hannah gasped. Indeed, it was beautiful.

"Shua," Taphath ordered the maid, "help the bride." Hannah removed her robe and allowed the maid to dress her in the purple gown. Longer than a nomad woman's robe, it hung down to cover her boots. Gently she touched the golden threads at the neckline.

"And here's your head covering." Elkanah's mother held up a white shawl woven from soft goat's wool.

"First I must braid her hair," Abia insisted. Slowly and with loving deliberation she fashioned Hannah's dark hair into a long braid that reached to her waist. Then Taphath draped the shawl over Hannah's head. Again she reached into the basket and brought out leather sandals. Hannah pulled off her boots and the maid replaced them with the sandals.

"And now the veil," Taphath announced.

Abia held up her hand. "I have prepared the veil." From a saddlebag she took a loosely-woven linen veil. Five small silver disks hung on the threads. Tears of gratitude threatened to overflow Hannah's eyes. Her mother had fashioned a traditional nomadic veil, and now she placed it over her daughter's face so only her eyes were visible.

A loud voice outside the tent announced, "The bridegroom and his guests come!" The two mothers peeked out the door, but clasping her hands tightly together, the bride waited in the center of the room. She heard determined footsteps and then Caleb's cordial voice rang out. "Welcome, bridegroom and gentlemen guests."

"I have come for my bride." At the sound of his voice her heart began to pound.

"Come out, daughter," Caleb called.

With the two mothers following behind her she emerged from the tent. In the twilight Elkanah stepped forward and held out his hand. Hannah caught her breath. How handsome he looked in his new black and white woolen robe! She placed her hand in his. Carefully her father removed the veil from Hannah's face, laid it across Elkanah's shoulder, and pronounced his blessing. "May you become the father of thousands."

The bride and groom turned toward Ramah and walked side by side across the wide pasture toward the city gate. Caleb and Jabal, Abia and Taphath, and all the wedding guests trailed behind them. Each guest carried a small clay lamp with a burning wick to give honored light for the marriage procession. Hannah glanced back once at the young women she had chosen for bridesmaids. She wished that Peninnah were among them, but the girl had refused her invitation.

A guard swung open the city's heavy bronze gate, and another guard waited a few paces ahead at the inner wall. From there a ramp led past shops to the upper terraces. Near the top of the hill the procession paused in front of a house. A large manservant opened the gate and bowed to the bride and groom. Hannah followed Elkanah into a stone-paved courtyard where torches set in the walls gave light. Two donkeys and a few sheep and goats rested on the far side of the courtyard. The smell of roasting lambs permeated the cool air.

Hannah had time for only a quick glance at a large, domed oven with a tall chimney and behind it the shadowed doorways to inner rooms before Elkanah directed her to an inside stone stairway that led to an upper room with a table set for the banquet. Elkanah's mother pointed to thick bolsters and cushions near the back wall. "Here is your place of honor to oversee the festivities." Caleb, Jabal, and some of the male guests filed in and seated themselves on the floor around the table. Laughing and chattering, other guests and Hannah's mother crowded into the room to sit on cushions.

Taphath disappeared into another room and quickly reappeared with a large shawl. She placed it around her son's shoulders and looked at Hannah. "A Levite must receive a prayer shawl on his wedding day. As required, I have woven it from unbleached lamb's wool." She held her hand under the wide fringe. "And see, in each corner I've braided in one blue thread." Continuing to explain she quoted from tradition, "The blue thread resembles the sea. The sea resembles the heavens. And the heavens resemble the Throne of Glory."

In deep respect Elkanah answered with a traditional prayer for such an occasion. "How precious is Your lovingkindness, O God, and the children of men take refuge in the shadow of Your wings."

Hannah touched the warmth of the cream-colored shawl. *Perhaps Taphath will teach me how to make lovely shawls and robes,* she mused.

Hired cooks brought roasted lamb to Elkanah. He cut a generous piece and placed it on a plate in front of his bride. And then the festivities began with pomegranates, dates, figs, pistachios, honey, bread, and wine added to the feast. From time to time the guests who had eaten left the table to make room for the next group. After all the men were satisfied, the women ate.

Late in the night Elkanah's mother whispered something to the young, unmarried women. With smiles and giggles they left the cushions and stood in front of Hannah. "We're ready to escort you to your chamber." Along with Taphath and Abia they led her to another upper room. After they had placed lamps on flat stone shelves that protruded from the walls, Hannah looked around the room. The bed was a comfortable platform covered with sheepskins, woolen blankets, and soft cushions. An acacia wood chest and several wicker baskets rested on the floor, tapestries covered the lower sections of the walls, and bright coals burned on the limestone hearth.

Taphath and Abia ushered the women out of the room and closed the heavy oak door behind them. Now alone, Hannah stood on a thick brown and white rug for a few minutes. Then she crawled onto the bed and waited for her husband to come.

Chapter 6

꧁꧂

*T*he voices of young boys echoing from the courtyard were the first sounds Hannah heard in the
morning. She turned over and became aware that
Elkanah had already left their bed. The security of his
warmth next to her was gone. But of course, he must teach
his students. She heard them troop into a lower room.

Other sounds floated up to her . . . the manservant
opening the gate for the shepherd who arrived to take
the sheep, goats, and donkeys to pasture . . . and then
footsteps outside her door. Elkanah's mother entered the
room. "I've brought a robe for you."

Hannah sat up and held out her hands for the white
woolen garment. After slipping into it, she stood and
smiled at her mother-in-law. "It's warm, just right to
wear on this cool autumn day."

When Taphath left the room to prepare for the second
day of the seven-day marriage celebration, Hannah
pushed aside a sheepskin covering and looked out a
small window. Dark rain clouds hovered over the mountains. She could see her clan's tents clustered beyond the
edge of Ramah's pasture. A solitary woman carrying a
bundle now walked across it toward the city and after
entering the gate, was lost to view. "My mother!"
Hannah exclaimed. "Coming to see me?"

Fastening on sandals, she descended to the courtyard
where the young servant girls Shua and Keren were

sweeping the stone floor. Hannah peered out the gate and saw her mother hurrying up the narrow street. Shua ran across the courtyard to unbar the gate.

Together Hannah and her mother climbed the stairs and entered the room. Abia glanced from the thick rugs to the tapestries to the acacia wood chest and let out a heavy sigh. "At last our daughter is a settler as your father wished."

"At least I can still look out windows and see pasture and mountains," Hannah replied.

Her mother shook her head. "Not pasture for nomads. I'm here to tell you that your father says we can't stay for the rest of your marriage celebration. There's not enough pastureland for our animals. We must leave this place today."

"Today?" Hannah echoed.

Abia held out the bundle. "I've brought your brown robe and your boots."

Gently Hannah accepted them from her mother. For a moment she gazed at her nomadic clothing and then at the robe she now wore. Her two lives were beginning to blend . . . a brown robe and boots for walking in the fields . . . a creamy-white robe and sandals to wear inside the house. "Thank you, Mother."

In silence they descended the stairs to the courtyard. At the gate they embraced briefly, and then Hannah watched her mother walk down the street toward the city wall. Later she looked again out the window. Her clan's black goathair tents had disappeared. A cat padded silently into the room and rubbed against her legs, apparently having wandered in from the street. The townspeople tolerated them because of the mice they caught—mice that would otherwise destroy their stores of grain. Hannah reached down and touched its soft fur.

Six more days of feasting completed the marriage festivities, and then the household settled into its usual routine. In the kitchen area storage jars held wheat, barley, lentils, sesame seeds, and olive oil. Bunches of garlic and onions hung from ceiling beams. Hannah learned to kindle a fire in the domed oven and when it glowed with heat, to remove the coals and place loaves of bread in the hot chamber. Some days she heated a clay pan and baked flat, unleavened bread—a reminder of her heritage, the nomadic life.

In the afternoons she waited for the shepherd to bring the animals from pasture. When she ventured into their shelter by the courtyard, Elkanah's donkeys learned to trust her. One at a time they nuzzled their heads under her arm while she scratched their backs and the sides of their necks.

During the evening as she and her husband sat together by the fire and at night when she lay near him, she could hear rain falling into the courtyard, yet the stone roof and Elkanah's warm embrace kept her secure. Even her fears of a fierce Philistine attack lessened. But each time the way of women came upon her, another concern grew. When would she be able to give her husband the son he deserved?

One day while Hannah was removing loaves from the oven, Taphath entered the kitchen with a length of white woolen cloth in her hands. "We must start sewing baby clothes," she announced.

"But only four moons have passed since my marriage," Hannah protested, trying to convince herself as well as her mother-in-law that no problem existed.

"Never too early to start sewing." Taphath produced a bone needle and woolen thread from a pocket in her sleeve. "You'll want your sons to be well-dressed."

Fighting against pangs of inadequacy, Hannah sat down on a bench. She watched as her mother-in-law spread out the fabric and, using a sharp bronze knife, cut the outline of a small robe. She threaded the needle and placed stitches around the neck of the garment.

"I've never seen such a delicate needle," Hannah exclaimed, "and such tiny stitches."

Taphath held out the sewing. "Here. Try it."

Hannah accepted the soft warm wool, the smooth needle. The thought of a son wearing the little robe brought a smile to her face. Under the older woman's direction, she learned to take neat stitches and soon stored finished baby garments in the acacia wood chest. Taphath ordered a carpenter to construct a loom for Hannah and place it in the large kitchen area. There by the warmth of the stove she wove white wool into baby blankets.

Winter rains gave way to gentle spring breezes. One morning wearing her brown robe and goatskin boots, Hannah ventured outside the city gates to the pasture. Perched in a carob tree, sparrows called out their lively songs. Near an outcropping of stone, blue violets lifted their dainty heads. One of Elkanah's donkeys ambled over and pressed his nose against Hannah's arm. Absently she rubbed her hand between his ears but her thoughts drifted. Although seven moons had now passed since her marriage, she was still failing to produce a son for Elkanah. A tear escaped from her eye and fell onto the donkey's head.

When she returned to the house, Hannah confided to her mother-in-law, "Maybe I'll never have a baby. Seven moons already and still no sign that I'm expecting a son for my husband."

Taphath stopped kneading bread and a sympathetic expression spread over her face. "I had the same problem. After my marriage, two years passed before I gave birth to Elkanah."

For a moment Hannah stared at her mother-in-law without speaking. Then she smiled. "You've given me some hope."

But as more moons passed, her smile faded, and she went about her daily activities in silence. All through the summer when they walked together in the fields and in the autumn when they sat by the kitchen fire, Elkanah tried to reassure her of his love. "How can you want me for your wife when I have failed you?" she asked.

"I love you for yourself, not for what you can do for me," he replied.

When time for the harvest festival drew near, Hannah struggled to overcome her anxiety. Soon they would travel to Shiloh, and there she would have to face her parents and confess that she had no son. And what would Peninnah say?

The morning for the journey dawned bright and clear. Hannah helped the maidservants load the donkeys. The hired shepherd arrived to stay in the house, and then Elkanah with all who lived in his household passed through Ramah's gates and journeyed toward the mountains. All day they trudged north along the ridges. By evening the small caravan stopped at an inn and slept comfortably on beds of straw.

Early in the morning they climbed along the road through the mountains. Hannah glanced often toward the south, looking for her clan's caravan, but she had already unloaded the donkeys at Shiloh before she saw her father leading his people toward their booths. A few moments later Abia stood before her, and Hannah's words tumbled out. "I have no son to show you."

"I have come to greet you, not inquire about a son,"

her mother replied, yet Hannah detected disappointment in her eyes.

At that moment Peninnah dashed to the booth. "Where's your son?"

"Maybe next year." Hannah looked toward the tabernacle and breathed a silent prayer. *Lord, help me.*

All through the week of worship and feasting her heart sank lower and lower until on the last day her husband said, "It troubles me that you are so sad."

"I've given you no heir," was her simple reply. He placed a generous portion of boiled lamb in her bowl and gently remarked, "We must thank the Lord that we have each other."

As the years passed Hannah often remembered his words and gave thanks for the kindness of her husband. But still, unable to produce a son for him, she continued to grieve. Three times each year Elkanah journeyed to Shiloh in order to worship and sacrifice to God, but Hannah and Taphath and the servants accompanied him only to the harvest festival. One year as Hannah packed a donkey she wondered, *Now that so many years have passed since my marriage, will anyone still ask me whether I have a son? Last year no one inquired—not even Peninnah.*

The two-day journey brought them to Shiloh before Caleb and the clan arrived. Elkanah had already cut branches to repair his booth and Hannah was gathering wood from under the teribinth oak trees when the caravan appeared from the north. She watched it wind among the booths until the people found their usual places. As she continued picking up dry twigs, she became aware of someone scuffing through the dry oak leaves. Looking up she saw Peninnah walking toward her.

The young woman stopped and leaned against a tree trunk. Tears ran down her cheeks and distress sobbed from her throat. Hannah dropped the twigs she was gathering. "What is it?"

Peninnah pulled aside the neck of her robe to reveal a dark bruise on her shoulder. "My father still beats me. He says I have to marry a settler but he never finds one for me. I'm not even promised."

Sympathy for her childhood friend flooded over Hannah. "I wish I could help you."

"You can. Find a husband for me in Ramah."

After a moment's hesitation Hannah offered, "I'll . . . I'll ask Elkanah if he knows someone."

A thin smile formed on Peninnah's lips. "You've made a promise."

At the end of the week as Hannah followed Elkanah homeward, she pondered, *How can I help Peninnah escape from her father's abuse?* An answer came slowly. Peninnah needed a husband. Elkanah needed a son. But the thought of sharing her home and husband with a second wife caused a shudder to tremble through Hannah's shoulders.

All during the winter and as spring and summer passed, she weighed the possibility. Sometimes she lay awake at night, mulling over what changes a second wife would cause in the household. At last one autumn day she mustered enough courage to bring the suggestion to Elkanah. They were strolling in the pasture when she took a deep breath and calmly stated, "Have you considered taking a second wife?"

He slowed his pace, but before he could answer, she blurted, "A man should have a son. No, not just one. Many sons to carry on his family traditions." There! She had said it, and a sense of relief washed over her.

Elkanah paused and took her hand in his. "Family traditions." For a long moment he gazed into her eyes. "If," he began, "just if I decide to take a second wife, would you help me choose the woman?"

Looking down at her boots, Hannah hesitated and then softly replied, "Yes, I could help."

Hand in hand they wandered farther into the meadow. When they started back toward the city, she had somehow found sufficient inner strength to suggest, "I'm sure my friend Peninnah would be happy as your wife."

"You are a kind and gentle person. But Peninnah?"

Hannah looked across the meadow to the distant hills. "Perhaps she could learn kindness from a thoughtful husband."

He too gazed into the distance. "I'll consider her."

A few days later as they journeyed toward Shiloh, Hannah confided to her mother-in-law. "I have suggested to Elkanah that he take a second wife."

Taphath nodded her head. "A wise decision. You have done what is right."

Have I? Hannah wondered. *Is this right? Especially if he takes Peninnah?*

Chapter 7

*A*t Shiloh Hannah watched for any indication that her husband planned to speak to Peninnah's father, but instead noticed him conferring with men from the tribes of Judah, Dan, and Benjamin. Disturbing rumors circulated throughout the encampment, and a chain of fear began to bind each tribe to the others. Many Philistine ships continued to sail across the great western sea toward the land of Israel, bringing more of their men, women, and children to settle the coastal lands. Those Philistines who had been longer in the land began to push up from the coastal Philistine cities into the Israelite hill territory.

The last night of the festival Hannah huddled under her blankets in the open booth. She lay awake long after Taphath on one side of her and Elkanah on the other breathed deeply in sleep. A slender trail of smoke from the dying campfire drifted over them, leaving its dark wood smell. A short distance away a donkey brayed and sheep answered with disturbed bleats. Was a hungry jackal circling the flocks?

In the morning as Hannah packed the donkeys, her husband reported to her, "I have spoken with the woman's father and . . ." Before he could tell her more, she heard a thin cry of pain. Peninnah's father pushed his daughter toward Elkanah and thrust her to the ground at his feet. "Take her today," the man growled. "Now that you've given me the bride price, take her. No need to wait for a year's betrothal time."

Elkanah reached down and helped her to her feet. Stepping between her and the angry father, he spoke in a firm voice. "As of this moment she is no longer yours." Hannah glanced at Peninnah and detected a smile flickering on the younger woman's lips.

All during the two-day march to their home a question kept going through Hannah's mind. *How long will it take me to adjust to sharing my husband with a second wife?* Yet Elkanah must have sons, she reminded herself as she tried to shake a feeling of anxiety that would not go away.

The sun was sinking behind the western hills and Ramah was a dark silhouette against the sky when the weary travelers approached its walls. They trudged up the hill and the hired shepherd unbarred the gate. Peninnah glanced around the courtyard. "So this is what my house and my courtyard look like," she exclaimed in happy excitement. "I'll fill it with sons for my husband."

Taphath took hold of her second daughter-in-law's arm and led her to the stairway. "But not yet. Tonight you will sleep in my room away from his on the lower floor."

Peninnah's shrill voice cut into the cool evening air. "I'll sleep in yours tonight, but then I want a room near my husband's." Reluctantly she followed Taphath to the upper floor.

While Shua and Keren unpacked the donkeys, and Elkanah inspected his sheep and goats, Hannah set out bread and cups of warm milk. *Why should Peninnah have a room so close to his?* she brooded. *It's only proper for a woman to have her chamber on the upper floor.*

The wedding celebration lasted for the required seven days. To keep her mind occupied with thoughts other than sharing her husband, Hannah helped the hired cooks bake bread and roast lambs. In the still hours of the night her bed felt cold and empty without Elkanah to share it with her as he so often did. How quickly the seven days of her own wedding had passed. But how slowly these days of Peninnah's celebration. At last the time ended.

Winter arrived, and the women spent most of their time in the warmth of the kitchen. On the shortest day of the year Peninnah stood in front of Elkanah's mother and announced, "Before next year's harvest festival, I will have a son." With an elated glint in her eyes, she turned and looked directly at Hannah.

And so it was. At the end of summer Taphath sent for a midwife and after an easy labor, Peninnah gave birth to a son. As the midwife cleansed the newborn and swaddled him in cloths, conflicting emotions heaved inside Hannah . . . bittersweet satisfaction that Elkanah had an heir to carry on his family traditions . . . heartache because she had failed to provide this child for him herself.

Peninnah named her son Othniel. As the years passed she gave birth to three more sons, a daughter, and then another son. The morning after the birth of the sixth child, Hannah entered the new mother's room to take care of her needs. Peninnah looked at her and scoffed, "What time do you expect your sons from their lessons?" Hannah stared at her in painful silence.

"You've been married to my husband for so long, surely you must have sons. Where are you hiding them?"

Glancing into the courtyard, Hannah saw Peninnah's younger children playing there. Not knowing what to say, she turned and walked out of the room.

Later that day at the time of the evening meal Taphath hobbled into the house and with a painful groan sank onto a bench. Elkanah rushed to her side. "Mother, are you ill?"

"Not ill. Just tired. I fear I can no longer endure the long journey to Shiloh and sleep in a booth. This year when you go to Sukkot, I will stay at home."

"I'll buy another donkey so you can ride," he offered.

"No. I must stay here by the hearth in my room."

The Feast of Ingathering without her mother-in-law? Hannah grasped the gray-haired woman's hand but was unable to speak.

On the way to Shiloh Hannah felt an emptiness without Taphath in the caravan. Even at their booth the loneliness persisted. She knelt by the hearth to add branches to the fire under the large pot of boiling lamb. Would her own mother come this year? The clan now often failed to appear, preferring to stay close by the River Jordan away from the threat of the Sea People.

As Hannah was laying out bowls, a man rushed to her fire. He thrust a long three-pronged fork into the pot and speared a leg of lamb.

She stared in amazement. "What are you doing with my meat?" she gasped.

The man laughed and, as he dashed away, yelled, "Phinehas and Hophni want their portion now." Disgusted, Hannah headed for the pasture where Elkanah was talking with several other Levites.

"Hophni and Phinehas' servant took part of our meat before we could offer it as sacrifice," she fumed. "They're supposed to serve God, not steal from others. What can we do?"

Her husband frowned. "Nothing. We have no right to chastise priests. Only the high priest can."

"Then you must tell Eli."

"We Levites have already spoken to him about his sons' behavior," he replied sadly, "but Eli has done nothing."

Together they walked back to their fire, and Elkanah gazed into the pot of lamb. He chose another leg to take to the high priest.

After the evening sacrifice Peninnah rested in the booth by the side of her newest baby while Hannah watched the other children play with small stones and bits of wood. She lifted the pot of remaining lamb from the fire and placed it on the ground between the rugs. Peninnah's children plopped down onto the rugs and their mother roused herself from the booth.

Elkanah forked meat and poured broth into bowls for his wives and children. When Peninnah glanced at the generous portion in Hannah's bowl, she whispered, "I see he's given you enough for all your sons."

Tearing her gaze from the expression on Peninnah's face, Hannah stared up at the dark sky. Tears blurred her vision, then, placing her bowl on the ground, she rushed toward the booth. Sinking to her knees she held her hands over her face and bowed her head to the earth.

A touch on her shoulder startled her. Elkanah knelt and his strong arms encircled her. "Hannah, why do you weep? And why do you not eat?" She raised her head and laid it against his warm shoulder.

"No son," was all she could say.

He held her close and gently comforted her. "Why is your heart sad? You have my love. Am I not more to you than ten sons?"

"You provide much for me, but I want to give sons to you."

Elkanah took her arm. "Come now and eat." He guided her back to the rugs and handed the bowl to her. After dipping bread into the broth she found herself still unable to swallow. "I must pray at the tabernacle."

He put down his bowl. "I'll go with you."

"I wish to go alone." She drew her shawl over her head and hurried in the shadowy twilight to enter the city gate. It felt strange to walk alone in the street and climb the stone stairway to the tabernacle courtyard. At the sight of the holy tabernacle she slowed her pace and approached it in reverent silence. A torch gave light near a doorpost, and Hannah advanced toward it.

Raising her head to look at the heavens she prayed in her heart, *O Lord of Hosts, to which host do I belong? If the heavenly, then I will never die. If to the mortal,* she argued, *I should be able to give birth. Of all the hosts You have created, is it so hard to give me a son?*

Suddenly ashamed of her outburst, she let her head droop. With determined effort she raised it again and silently pleaded, *If You will indeed look on the affliction of Your handmaid and remember me, and not forget Your handmaid, but will give Your handmaid a male child, then I will give him to the Lord all the days of his life, and no razor shall come upon his head.*

Without warning the high priest's stern voice broke into her prayer and demanded, "How long will you be drunk? Put away your wine!"

Startled, Hannah stepped backward. "No, my lord, I have drunk neither wine nor strong drink," she protested. "I am a woman sorely troubled and have been pouring out my soul before the Lord. Do not regard your maidservant as a base woman for I have been speaking out of my great anxiety and grief."

In the light from the torch Eli studied her face. "I observed your lips moving but no sound came out. You claim you were praying. To me you appear to have drunk too much new wine."

"No, no, my lord, I am not drunk," she insisted, "and because you have accused me of something I have not done, you must bless me."

A sad tone came into Eli's voice. "I have seen too much drunkenness at these festivals. But you speak the truth. I have suspected you unjustly and am obligated to bless you." He raised his right hand. "Go in peace, and may the God of Israel grant the petition which you have asked of Him."

Briefly she stared at him, and then shivering from deep emotion and the evening chill, she drew her shawl more tightly around her head. The courtyard lay dark before her as she walked cautiously across its stones. As she passed the large altar a figure arose from behind it and confronted her. "I can guess why you are troubled," the voice of Eli's son Hophni grated on her ears. "You've failed your husband." He stepped forward and grabbing her around the waist, he pulled her to him. "If you want sons, come lie in the tabernacle with me. I can provide them for you."

She pushed her fists against his chest and kicked his shins. With a curse he released his hold on her, and she dashed toward the stairway. Hophni's harsh laughter followed her. Halfway down the stairs she heard footsteps from below. Had she anguished at the tabernacle so long that a Levite was already starting to lead pilgrims to the courtyard for evening worship? But she heard no singing, no timbrels, no drums. Could it be Eli's other son Phinehas? Stepping off the stairway onto the rocky hillside, she crouched, hoping whoever ascended would pass without seeing her.

The footsteps came nearer and then she heard her husband's gentle voice. "Hannah." With a sob of relief she threw herself into his arms.

"Because you were so troubled, I came to find you."

"Thank you for your concern, but I went to the tabernacle to pray for a son. The high priest found me, and he asked the Lord to grant my petition. Now I'm no longer sad."

Elkanah raised his voice. "Praise to the Lord." With his steady hand on her arm, they descended the stairway and returned to their fire.

Her youngest son in her arms, Peninnah emerged from the booth and stared at Hannah in the dim light. "Why are you smiling?"

"I have begged the Lord to give me a son."

"Huh!" Peninnah huffed. "When?"

"Some day." Hannah sat down by the fire and took up her bowl. As she dipped bread into the broth, doubt began to creep into her mind. *All these years I have wanted a son but it has been a joy denied me. Will it really happen now? Will God heed the high priest's blessing?* A second concern caused her to stop eating. Eventually she must tell her husband that if she did indeed produce a son, she must dedicate him to the Lord.

Chapter 8

ᕫᔪᔪᔪᕫ

Raindrops splashed onto Hannah's face. This last night of the festival she had slept lightly, wakening often to ponder how to tell Elkanah of her bargain with God. Her husband stirred by her side in the booth and wiped the rain from his face. "We must worship early so we can pack and leave for home. This year we have only one day to travel before the Sabbath overtakes us at sundown. If we start soon, we can cover the entire distance."

"Two days' journey in one?" Hannah questioned as she thought how Peninnah would complain.

"With this rainstorm blowing from the west, many travelers will have to seek lodging, and we would have difficulty finding room in an inn. Come, let us take our offering to the Lord and then begin our journey."

Quickly she placed pomegranates and dates in a basket and then followed Elkanah through the dark camp. They hurried up the mount to the tabernacle where just a few hours earlier Hannah had prayed. Now no torches held back the darkness.

While her husband entered the sanctuary to leave his offering, she waited outside near the tabernacle's doorposts. The memory of Hophni's arm around her waist made her shudder. With a son so evil, could Eli's words ever come true? A wave of doubt washed over her. Did the old priest's blessing really come from God? She tried to shake away her uncertainty while she gazed through the dark rain toward the first token of eastern light.

Soon Elkanah emerged from the tabernacle, and they hastened across the courtyard and down the stairway to their booth. Hannah touched Peninnah's arm. "Wake up. Elkanah is bringing the donkeys."

The younger wife turned over and grumbled, "Why are you making me get up so early?" Her youngest son started to cry.

"We must pack and leave." Hannah picked up the baby and comforted him against her shoulder. "We're traveling all the way to Ramah before sundown." Still muttering, Peninnah crawled out from under her blankets and roused the other children from sleep.

All day in steady rain they plodded homeward, not even stopping for a midmorning meal. While they walked, they broke bread and passed it along with fresh dates to the children. The time of sunset caught them in the pasture outside Ramah, but claiming their right to a Sabbath Day's journey of 2000 cubits, they passed into the city and climbed the hill to their home.

Less than two moons later Hannah entered her mother-in-law's room to serve bread and milk. The grayhaired woman, wrapped in a blanket, sat close to the fire. "These winter winds send a chill through me," she said slowly.

Hannah handed a cup of hot milk to her. "I have news that will warm your heart."

"What can that be?"

"You shall have another grandson."

"You mean Peninnah . . ."

"No. I will give you this grandson. When we worshiped at Shiloh, I prayed, and the Lord has answered my petition."

A look of disbelief flitted across Taphath's face. Then

she put down her cup and threw off the blanket. "Dear daughter," she exclaimed, embracing Hannah, "you have given me hope and joy. Praise to our God for allowing this great happiness in my life."

"Your son is also highly pleased."

"As he should be."

Hannah heard the boys from Elkanah's scribal school scattering out the courtyard gate to race toward their homes for the midmorning meal. "I will go now to serve my husband."

Elkanah met her in the courtyard. Together they sat by the hearth to take their bread and warm milk. Hannah hesitated to speak about the burden on her mind, but she determined to wait no longer. "I must tell you more about my prayer at Shiloh."

He laid his hand on hers. "I remember you were so distressed you couldn't eat."

"That's when I promised the Lord that if He gave me a son, I would dedicate the child to Him. After our son is weaned, I'll have to take him to Shiloh and leave him at the tabernacle."

Elkanah's grip on her hand tightened, and he remained in deep thought for several moments before giving his controlled reply. "I will find it hard to give up this special son. But when we make promises to God, we must keep them."

Hannah sighed in gratitude for her understanding husband, yet she couldn't bring herself to look at Peninnah who had entered the courtyard cooking area just as Hannah confessed her promise. She must have overheard.

All through the time of budding hyacinths and flowering almond trees Hannah lived in grateful anticipation . . . often touching her rounded figure and telling the unborn child, "I love you, my baby."

"You'll never catch up with me," Peninnah taunted her one day. "I may be my husband's second wife but I provided his firstborn son."

Yet the younger woman's hostility failed to dim Hannah's happiness. "Elkanah can love many sons," she replied.

"What if it's a daughter?"

"I have the Lord's blessing. This child is a son."

Many times she thought of her mother and yearned to talk with her, to ask questions, to seek advice, to share the joy, but Abia was far away by the River Jordan.

During the warm summer Hannah wove lengths of swaddling clothes from soft white wool, and as the first leaves of the oak trees began to fall, her time drew near. One morning she was in the cooking area of the courtyard mixing ground lentil and honey cakes when the blare of trumpets and loud shouting exploded in the street. A shaft of alarm pierced her breast.

The maid Shua dashed into the kitchen. "Philistines! Marching toward Ramah."

The school boys, shrieking in fright, raced out the courtyard gate. Elkanah appeared with a sword buckled to his waist and a short spear in his right hand. "Everyone stay in the house," he ordered. "I'm going to the outer wall."

No, don't go, Hannah wanted to scream, yet she knew he must help defend the city. He and his manservant headed out the gate, and Shua barred it securely. A few minutes later the hired shepherd shouted from the street that he had brought Elkanah's donkeys, sheep, and goats. The maid helped him push the animals into the courtyard before he dashed away. Then all was quiet. Too quiet. No more racing footsteps in the street. In the kitchen area no one spoke. The lentil and honey cakes, ready to fry, lay uncooked on a tray.

Hannah's mind pictured the men of Ramah, some with spears, others with bows and arrows, crouching behind the stone parapets on the top of the city wall. She ventured into the courtyard and hurried to Peninnah's room. "May this one come in?" she asked.

Peninnah huddled with her brood of children under blankets on the bed. "Where can we hide?" she wailed.

Trying to reassure herself as well as the younger woman, Hannah replied, "The thick walls and our brave men will protect us."

"But my mother always told me Philistines have long spears and big, straight swords. They'll break down our city gates and swarm into the streets. When they enter our house, they'll . . ."

"Our men will chase them away from the gates."

"They can't," Peninnah cried. "Not on foot against the Philistines with their horses and chariots." The children clung to her and sobbed in fear.

A sudden cramp caused Hannah to wince. She bent over and pressed her hands against her full abdomen.

Peninnah sat up. "You have pain?"

"I must go to my room." She stumbled across the courtyard and struggled up the stairway to her bed.

A few moments later Peninnah entered the room accompanied by Elkanah's mother and the two maids. Hannah groaned as another contraction wrung her. "Keren," Taphath commanded, "go for the midwife."

"It's not possible," Peninnah informed the older woman. "My husband ordered all of us to stay in the house, and we can't go against his word. I will deliver the child."

"You?" Taphath protested. "You've never delivered a baby."

"I've given birth to many," she answered, lifting her

chin arrogantly. "I know what happens when a child is born."

Hannah closed her eyes and wondered, *But can I trust her with my child?* Another contraction, harder than before, brought a small cry to her lips.

"I'll bring the swaddling clothes," Taphath offered.

Peninnah spoke to the maids. "I need sesame oil and salt." She paused before adding, "We have no birthing stool. What can we use?"

Shua and Keren remained silent, unable to think of anything. "Find some pieces of fleece for her to squat over," Peninnah ordered. "Go and bring everything I'll need." She followed them out to once more comfort her children.

Alone in the room Hannah listened to deep thuds that echoed all the way from the city walls at the foot of the hill. The Philistines were battering against the gates and walls while the men of Ramah dropped heavy stones onto the invaders. Horses neighed in the midst of the tumult. If the attackers tried to place scaling ladders against the walls, she knew that archers would shoot arrows straight down upon them. Hannah trembled at the realization that the enemy had already advanced so close. "Lord, protect Elkanah," she whispered.

More pain seized her, and she moaned in agony. When Taphath brought the swaddling clothes, she sat close to the bed and began to offer words of encouragement. In a regular rhythm the pain rose to excruciating strength before ebbing away. Between each contraction Hannah heard the noise of battle at the city walls.

Peninnah returned and scolded her. "You're resisting instead of helping. Relax your face and hands and let the rest of your body do the work. That's what the midwife always tells me."

"Why must I give birth without a midwife?" Hannah

groaned as Elkanah's mother patted her hand. Then with a feeling of downward movement, Hannah screamed, "The baby's coming."

Quickly the maids helped her to squat over the fleece on the floor. In a rush of water the infant emerged into Peninnah's waiting hands. Her voice was barely audible as she announced, "You have a son." Grasping the baby's feet, she held him upside down to cleanse the mucous from his mouth. His loud cry brought squeals of delight from Keren and Shua.

Using strands of linen yarn Peninnah tied the cord in two places, cut between them with a bronze knife, and handed the baby to Keren. The maid cleansed him with warm sesame oil, and to toughen his skin, rubbed him gently with salt.

Still squatting on the floor, Hannah looked up at her well-formed infant, and tears of happiness filled her eyes. "My son." She formed the soft words with her dry lips. "At last I have a son for Elkanah. Thank You, Lord."

Shua helped her return to the bed and into a clean tunic. Keren placed the swaddled infant by her side, and the new mother slipped her arm under the baby's head to draw him close. His black hair was damp, and he bore the comforting, seed-harvest smell of the gentle sesame oil. Pulling his little hand from under the clothes, she marveled at his tiny fingers. He opened his dark eyes and for a brief moment appeared to look at her. Hannah kissed his warm cheek and tried to put an everpresent reality out of her mind—the distressing thought that some day she must leave him at Shiloh.

Shouts from the city walls cruelly reminded her of the danger surrounding Ramah. Hugging her son closer, she murmured, "Lord, make the enemy retreat. Bring my husband here to see his son."

Taphath returned to her room and the maids to their chores, taking with them the soiled fleece. Peninnah gazed for a moment at the newborn and then with an exhausted sigh, left without saying anything. Hannah closed her eyes and allowed her tired body to remain completely still.

Late afternoon sunshine slanted into the room through the gap where the sheepskin window covering had been pulled aside. One of the town's half-wild cats padded softly into the room and sniffed curiously at the air. It jumped onto the bed and lay down at the foot where it could observe this new creature nestled next to Hannah.

Chapter 9

❦

When the baby whimpered, Hannah pulled aside her loose tunic and held him to her breast. He nuzzled it, searching instinctively for food.

A great shouting vibrated through the dusky air. The cat leaped off the bed and scurried out the door. Although Hannah stiffened, the child continued to nurse.

Shua rushed into the room and dashed to the window. "They're leaving. I can see them retreating." Her voice rose in excitement. "Our men have defeated the Philistines."

"Praise to the Lord," Hannah echoed the maid's joy. She looked again at her son. He had fallen asleep with his eyes tightly closed. "Find a boy in the street to take a message to the master of this household that a son has been born."

"Yes, mistress. I'll go right now."

Hannah closed her eyes and slept along with her baby. A gentle touch on her arm brought her back to consciousness. Someone had lit lamps in the room and by their light she could see a broad smile on her husband's face.

"You have done well, dear wife." Elkanah picked up his son and held him carefully in his capable hands. "Some time ago you spoke of naming our child Samuel. Is this still your wish?"

"Because I have asked him of the Lord, I want to

honor our holy God," she readily answered. Then she paused, searching her husband's face for his reaction. "Yes, I would like to give our son the name Samuel."

"It has power and strength, and it includes 'El' the name of God. I agree. He shall be called Samuel." Leaning over the bed, he carefully placed the baby by Hannah's side. As she looked up at Elkanah, his lips found hers for a reassuring kiss. "Now I must return to the wall," he said solemnly. With one last look at his sleeping son, he left the room.

Light from the clay lamps continued to flicker on the mud-plastered walls, yet the room seemed darker with her husband gone. In the city streets women lifted their mournful wail for the men of Ramah who had lost their lives in the battle.

Hannah pulled the blanket closer around herself and the baby. Sounds from the courtyard drifted up to her. A sheep bleated. Peninnah scolded a child who had strayed out of their room. Then Hannah recognized Keren's quick footsteps outside the door before the maid entered. "I have brought barley soup and some of the lentil and honey cakes for your evening meal."

Slowly Hannah sat up. "I am grateful for your help." She had taken only a few spoonfuls of soup when the baby woke up and demanded her breast. "You are strong and healthy, little man-child," she told him.

His lips held firmly to the nipple, and she craved to keep him with her forever, yet some day she must fulfill her promise. After he no longer needed nourishment from her, she would have to take him to Shiloh. A tear slipped from under her eyelid. She brushed it away and determined to cherish each moment she would have with her child.

As harvest time drew near, the days shortened and

they needed a fire continually on the hearths. Hannah resumed her duties of baking bread and caring for her mother-in-law.

A few days before the harvest festival Elkanah sat in the kitchen area for the evening meal with his wives and children when he announced, "Most of our men will stay in Ramah to protect the city in case the Philistines besiege us again, but my household must go to Shiloh."

"Please," Hannah implored, "this year your newest son is too young to travel. After he is weaned, I will bring him to the tabernacle so that he may appear in the presence of the Lord." With a catch in her voice she added, "And abide there forever."

Elkanah gazed at the infant in her arms. "Do whatever seems best to you. But wait until you have weaned him."

"What about the safety of my children?" Peninnah demanded. "What if Philistines attack us on our way, and we have nowhere to go for refuge?"

"I am a Levite, and we must go to Shiloh to worship," he answered firmly.

Hannah nestled her baby closer against her as Elkanah spoke again. "Some day all the tribes of Israel must forego their differences. We need to join forces to withstand the invading Philistines and other Sea Peoples."

"I don't trust any other tribe," Peninnah fretted.

"To save our land," Elkanah replied, "we will have to trust the tribes and depend upon our God to stay with us."

Finally the day of departure arrived. Hannah helped Peninnah load the donkeys with sheepskins, blankets, food, and children, and then watched Elkanah lead his little group out the courtyard gate. Shua trailed behind Peninnah to help her with the children.

Nathan, staying to protect those at home, returned to the servants' quarters, Keren to the kitchen area, and

Hannah—shivering slightly in the early morning chill—to her room.

The house remained strangely quiet. She missed the cheerful noise of children chasing each other around the courtyard, the familiar sound of boys reciting their lessons. Loneliness threatened to overwhelm her. On her fingers Hannah counted the days until her husband and the rest of the household would return. Picking up her son, she whispered to him, "Drink well and often, little one, so my milk will continue to flow and I can keep you close to me."

On the day when she expected the travelers to return home, dawn came without the usual autumn rain. Sunshine crept over the eastern mountains to brighten Ramah's pasture land. Hannah baked bread and its warm, yeasty smell invaded the courtyard and drifted to the upper rooms.

Many times during the day she drew aside the sheepskin to peer out her window. At last she spotted the small caravan approaching in the distance. Slowly it advanced to the city gates. Hannah waited with Keren by the door and Nathan by the gate until with weary footsteps Elkanah led his troop into the courtyard. The younger children slid off their perches atop the laden donkeys and huddled around the warm hearth. Nathan helped the maidservants unload the animals.

Peninnah confronted Hannah as she brought bread and bowls of stew. "You should have been there to see Hophni and Phinehas," she exclaimed.

Hannah dropped a loaf of bread to the floor. Why would she ever want to see Eli's degenerate sons?

The younger woman's eyes glowed with excitement. "They were worse than ever this year. You've seen their servants thrust big forks into the people's kettles of boiling lamb. Now they even sent their servants to take meat before it was cooked."

"How can they do such evil things?"

"I guess they're rebelling against their father." Peninnah's laughter filled the cooking area of the courtyard.

"Eli should stop them," Hannah insisted in outraged shock.

"Eli is growing old," Elkanah answered solemnly. "He's not able to control his sons."

A gasp escaped from Hannah, and she dashed to the stairway. In her room she picked up her sleeping son and held him close to her. "Why, Lord," she argued, "why must I leave this innocent child with an old man and his corrupt sons? Why are You asking me to do this?" Before she finished speaking, she knew the answer. God hadn't asked her to leave Samuel at the tabernacle. She had herself made the vow to dedicate him when she begged for a son. Some day she must take him to the high priest and trust in the Lord to protect him from any evil.

Time and again through the winter and summer Peninnah repeated her tale of Eli's sons, appearing to delight in the grief she caused to Hannah. One autumn morning as they warmed milk for the midmorning meal, Peninnah demanded, "Why are you not going to Shiloh again this year?"

"Samuel is too young for the journey."

"I always took my babies when they were his age, and the one I'm carrying now will go with me this year."

Hannah glanced at Peninnah's rounded abdomen and wished that she, too, might expect another child. "I will take Samuel after I wean him."

"You're just afraid that the high priest will see him and insist that you leave him there."

Her hands full of bread and a jug of milk for Elkanah's mother, Hannah left the room without answering Peninnah's barb. It was true. She was afraid.

Each year when the wood pigeons flew south and leaves fell from the oak trees, the younger wife badgered the older one, "When are you going to stop feeding that big boy?"

"Nomad women nurse their children until they're 4 years old."

"Of course, but you're no longer a nomad. You're a city dweller and should follow its customs."

"I will do what I think is best for my son." Then she added silently to herself, *And until I can bear to part with him.*

Few nomads pastured their flocks on the western side of the mountains. Fear of Philistine invasion kept them to the east, close to the River Jordan. Occasionally a wanderer happened into Ramah, bringing frightening tales of the Sea Peoples. They continued to fortify their captured cities of Ashdod, Ashkelon, and Ekron, strengthening the walls and building towers. In Ashdod they built a new house for Dagon, the god they had adopted from the Canaanites. "With my own eyes," Hannah heard one man speak in the marketplace, "I observed Philistines repairing their ships in the sea near Ashkelon. They've conquered the coast. When will they invade our mountains again?"

Hannah hurried home to report the news to her husband. Three-year-old Samuel ran out of the kitchen where he was playing with his stepbrothers. He had grown into a sturdy little boy with dark brown hair falling to his shoulders. When she knelt beside him, he threw his arms around her neck and hugged her tightly. She took his hand and led him to where his father taught his students. When Elkanah saw her anxious face, he listened to her tale.

"The tribes must join together and choose a strong leader to fight the Sea People," he repeated the opinion she had heard from him many times before. "Neither Ephraim nor Benjamin nor any tribe is strong enough alone to withstand an invasion without help from the others."

"A strong leader to fight the Sea People." The little boy jumped up and down echoing his father's words.

"Come, Samuel." Hannah steered the excited child up to her room. To calm him she sat on her bed and recited one of the stories that her mother had told her as a child. "We live in the land of Ephraim. It's named after a son of Joseph. Joseph was the son of Jacob, and Jacob the son of Isaac, the son of Abraham who came from a city called Haran in the northern country of Padam-Aram. God promised all the land where the tribes now live to Abraham and his descendants. When God makes a promise, He always keeps it, and we must do the same."

Instantly she closed her eyes, vividly remembering her promise. Samuel listened with interest. Before many days had passed she had repeated the story enough times that he could say it with her.

As he played with a small kitten in the courtyard late one afternoon, Hannah watched with a growing sadness in her heart. She cherished the expressions, so much like his father's, that crossed his face. "Samuel," she called. "Come to me now before the evening meal." Still holding the kitten, he stood by her side to nurse.

"Before too many days," she said a few minutes later, "you will have your fourth birthday. Each day this week you will drink less and less from me, and on your birthday you will stop."

His eyes brightened. "Does that mean I get to go to Shiloh with Father like my brothers do?"

"Yes, and I will go with you."

A frown creased the little boy's forehead. "Othniel and my other brothers say that if you take me to Shiloh, you're going to leave me, and I'll have to stay there forever. They're always teasing me." His voice rose in anger. "They tell me lots of things that aren't true. They're just teasing, aren't they?"

Chapter 10

I made a promise to God," Hannah explained, "and I must keep it."

Samuel dropped the kitten and stared at his mother. Then he flung himself onto the sheepskin-covered mat that was his small bed. The kitten pushed its nose against the boy's cheek.

"Samuel," Hannah called softly. When he sat up, she held out her arms to him. The little boy threw himself into her embrace. She hugged him against her breast with her tear-stained cheek on the top of his head. "I'll come to see you."

Too anguished to say more, she placed him onto his bed again and descended to where she had set up her loom. An unfinished robe stretched across the frame. She sat down and thrust the shuttle listlessly through the threads. Of brown and white stripes like the one Elkanah had worn when she first met him at Shiloh, this robe was for her son when she would leave him at the tabernacle. Already she had ordered the shoemaker to fashion leather boots for the boy.

And now the time drew near. With a heavy heart Hannah made preparations for her special offerings and sacrifice at Shiloh. She bought a goatskin of wine and a good supply of wheat. The maidservants labored to grind the wheat into large amounts of flour until they had enough to fill three tightly-woven linen bags. She accompanied Elkanah to the pasture where he bargained with a farmer for a fully-developed, 3-year-old bullock. Its hide was the color of earth, and the hump behind its neck added a sense of power.

Hannah waited under a grove of junipers at the edge of the pasture. "See how big and strong this one is," she heard the farmer shout. Although she could not hear Elkanah's quiet response, she knew he was offering a price and what he expected in return. "Yes, yes," the man's loud voice carried across the meadow, "I will leave the bronze ring hooked in its nose and the rawhide ropes fastened to it." Hannah watched him accept payment of bars and scraps of silver. Elkanah smiled as he returned to her. "He will keep the bullock here until the day we leave for Shiloh."

After Hannah baked bread for the journey, she helped Samuel pack his new robe and boots into a goatskin bag. Nathan brought the donkeys for the maidservants to load. Elkanah had hired a man he trusted as gatekeeper during the household's absence, and Keren would take her turn to stay with Taphath.

All the others set out from Ramah early one morning with the loaded donkeys and a lamb for their Sabbath Eve meal at the harvest festival. In the meadow the farmer waited for them with the bullock tethered to a stout stake. The animal lowered its head and glared at the approaching donkeys, lamb, and people. When Peninnah's children saw it, they yelped in fright and scurried to hide behind the donkeys. Hannah put her arm around Samuel. "Oh, big!" he said. "And its horns look sharp."

"Yes, big," she answered, realizing the bullock was larger than it had appeared when she viewed it across the pasture. "Stay away from it."

Cautiously Elkanah and Nathan pulled up the stake and took hold of the braided, rawhide ropes fastened through the bullock's nose ring. As they followed the narrow trail they walked on either side of the animal, keeping a firm tug on the ropes to encourage the bull forward. Their staffs in their hands, they watched carefully for any sign that it might become savage.

As Hannah and Samuel accompanied a donkey, she heard a faint sound, a plaintive meowing. She glanced at the roadside grass but soon realized the distressed call came from a goatskin bag on the donkey's back. Samuel's pleading eyes looked up at her. "I brought my kitten."

"Samuel!" She started to scold him but suddenly the remembrance of cats in her own childhood flowed over her—cats riding on loaded carts, cats crawling under her blankets, mother cats nursing their babies. She reached into the bag and brought out the frightened gray kitten. Samuel held up his hands to receive it.

Peninnah hurried forward. "You're not going to let that spoiled boy take his cat to Shiloh, are you? You know that many people consider them taboo around the tabernacle. Because the Egyptians worship them as gods."

"He shall take it. The Egyptians worship sheep and cattle, but we don't consider them taboo. Besides, he'll keep it away from the priests and the tabernacle."

"You should drop it here."

"No," Hannah answered firmly. "Samuel will keep it with him."

They heard Elkanah shout at the head of the little caravan. "Turn here. We've going into this town."

"Why?" Peninnah questioned. "We never stop this early in the day."

Before they reached the town gate, he halted his family to explain. "Too many of our people have always failed to make the pilgrimage to worship at Shiloh. Now with the constant fear of a Philistine attack, even less are taking the journey. We will pass slowly through the streets of several towns to arouse interest and encourage others to join us."

Peninnah groaned. "What if they become angry?"

"Don't be afraid. Our God travels with us." He turned to Nathan. "We'll tether the bullock here, and I will ask you to stay with it while I visit this town." He picked up a stone and used it to pound the stake into the ground. While Nathan held his staff ready, Elkanah tied the bullock's ropes to the stake.

Hannah took Samuel's hand. "Where's your kitten?"

He patted his stomach. "It's asleep in my robe pocket."

The first man they met in the city streets immediately asked Elkanah, "Where are you traveling with these women and children?"

"We're journeying to Shiloh to observe the holy celebration of Sukkot, the Feast of Ingathering. Come, join us, and you will be glad."

The man fingered his beard in concentration. "When my father was alive, he made the trip every year, but I have never gone to the festival since."

"Consider it," Elkanah urged. "God has commanded all of His people to go, and we must obey."

"I will consider it," the man answered.

Late in the afternoon as they approached another town, Hannah was relieved to see the inn where they planned to lodge for the night. The two-story limestone building looked over its section of the town wall. Elkanah led his caravan through the city gate and into the inn's large courtyard. The children helped carry the sheepskins, blankets, and goatskin bags up to a room on the second floor where all, including the lamb, would sleep. Elkanah tethered the donkeys in the courtyard and herded the bullock into a stone-walled pen.

In the bare room Elkanah's household seated themselves on their sheepskins and supped on barley loaves, brown goat cheese, and figs. While the others slept, Hannah lay awake with little Samuel breathing softly close by her side. Just this night and a few more remained for her to have him with her. The kitten crawled across the blanket and snuggled against her neck. At last she fell asleep.

The following day's journey was a steady climb up the steep mountain road. When they turned north onto the ancient patriarchal highway, Hannah reflected about the many times she had traveled to Shiloh—all through her girlhood and every year with her husband except when she had stayed home with Samuel. The little boy ran ahead, shouting to his father, "When do we get to see the tabernacle?"

Elkanah raised his staff and pointed ahead. "Look there." In the distance the sanctuary stood in quiet rest on the mount.

They descended to the valley floor and finally arrived at their booth. After Elkanah helped Nathan take the bullock and lamb to pasture, he ordered his older sons, "Come with me to gather cedar and myrtle. We need to enlarge our shelter."

The women and small children unloaded the donkeys, gathered firewood, and prepared a simple supper of bread and dates. As he finished eating, Elkanah announced, "On the last full day we are here, we will make our offerings of gratitude to the Lord." Hannah heard the sadness in his voice, and the words sent a chill through her. *The time is coming. The time is coming too soon.*

The days passed quickly. She watched her small son play with twigs she had gathered for the cooking fire. He arranged them to form a little booth in which he placed his kitten. It peered out at him but remained content in its makeshift shelter.

When he was not performing his Levitical duties, Elkanah spent time with Samuel. Hannah was always pleased to hear him say, "Come son, let us walk." Eagerly the boy took his father's hand, and they strolled to the vineyards, the meadows, the lower hills.

Other times she sat by the fire with Samuel and related family history. "When you live at the tabernacle, never forget that you are the son of Elkanah, a Levite assigned to the tribe of Ephraim, and your father is the son of Jeroham, the son of Elihu, the son of Tohu, the son of Zuph." Dutifully Samuel repeated the names.

The morning of the last full day, Hannah heated water to bathe her son and then she dressed him in his new brown and white striped robe and badgerskin boots. "Bring your goatskin bag," she told him. When he handed it to her, she explained, "I'm putting your other robe and boots, a blanket, and some pistachio nuts into your bag, and we'll take along a sheepskin for you to sleep on."

He pouted. "Is this the day you're going to leave me at the tabernacle?"

"Yes," she choked out the words, "this day I will fulfill my promise to the Lord."

The little boy glanced toward the tabernacle complex. High above it a few thin clouds drifted lazily across the sky. He picked up his kitten and pushed it into his goatskin bag. Pretending not to notice, Hannah combed her hair. A loud snort from the humpbacked bullock warned her that all was ready for the sacrifice.

Peninnah sat on a rug by the fire and coolly announced, "I shall remain here while you perform this unnecessary deed, and my children will stay here with me."

The children sent up a loud wail. "We want to go too."
"No!" she shouted at them.

Elkanah's calm voice broke into the argument. "We are a family, and all the family will help take the offerings." He pointed to his older boys. "You three will carry the bags of flour and you two the wineskin." Peninnah turned her face away but made no further objection.

With his staff in his hand Nathan led the bullock toward Shiloh. Levites from other booths strolled over and offered to carry some of the large amount of firewood that Hannah had gathered. As she picked up more wood and the sheepskin, Samuel grabbed his bag. Along with Shua also laden with wood and Peninnah carrying her newest baby, they followed the men and the bullock toward the city gate.

The familiar stone stairway up to the tabernacle courtyard took on a sudden strangeness for Hannah. She had not climbed it since that fateful night when she had made her rash promise to God. "Lord," she now prayed, "do not forsake me. Give me strength." The heavy sound of the bullock's hooves on the stones echoed into her heart. The courtyard appeared wider than she remembered, the altar higher.

Elkanah directed the children to the tabernacle where he took the wine and flour from them and laid it on the porch. The Levites heaped the wood on the large courtyard altar. Placing her hand on Samuel's shoulder, Hannah pulled him back to the edge of the courtyard while Elkanah beckoned for Nathan to bring the bullock. It bellowed loudly and struggled, then collapsed as the knife slit its throat. The other Levites helped Elkanah lift its body onto the leaping flames so the fire could begin to consume his offering of gratitude for giving him a son. Soon the smell of burning meat permeated the courtyard air.

Still clutching his bag, Samuel leaned against his mother. She gazed down at him. "Where's the old priest?" he asked.

At that moment Eli emerged from the tabernacle and demanded, "What is this sacrifice?"

Startled by his sudden appearance, Hannah raised her head. "Oh, my lord!" she cried out. "As you live, my lord, I am the woman who several years ago stood here in your presence, praying to the Lord. For this child I prayed, and the Lord has granted me my petition which I made to Him. Therefore I have dedicated him to the Lord. As long as he lives, he is dedicated to the Lord."

Eli stared at the little boy who solemnly gazed up at him. "Then you are leaving the child here with me?" the priest asked in surprise.

Her voice was a soft whisper. "Yes, and here is a sheepskin for him to sleep on."

As he took the sheepskin from her, a pensive smile softened the old man's face. "I have failed to teach my sons the ways of the Lord, but now He's giving me a new son to instruct," he said quietly. Looking down at the boy, he asked, "What is your name?"

"Samuel."

"Samuel, I will make a bed for you in the tabernacle."

A plaintive meowing sounded from the bag. The boy patted the goatskin and stepped closer to his mother. "What do you have in there?" Eli asked sternly.

"I have a blanket and some nuts." He hesitated before adding, "and my kitten."

The old priest let out a hearty chuckle. "We could use another cat. Too many mice. He can live where we store the grain," he said as he took Samuel's hand. With one last look at Hannah, her son passed into the tabernacle, a place she was not allowed to enter.

Chapter 11

❧❧❧

As Hannah stared at the closed portals, a feeling of desolation overwhelmed her. Her head drooped in despair for a moment, but then she quickly raised it toward the heavens. With trembling voice and thankful heart she prayed in adoration to God for giving her a son. "My heart rejoices in the Lord. There is none holy like the Lord, for there is none besides You, nor is there any rock like our God."

Her lengthy prayer continued until she heard Elkanah's footsteps behind her and felt his arm around her shoulders. "We leave our son in the Lord's hands," he said softly.

"When will we see him again?"

"God willing, at tonight's worship."

Slowly they walked away from the tabernacle, past the altar with its burning sacrifice, down the stone stairway, and through the city gate to their booth.

Peninnah had already returned to sit by the fire with her youngest son at her feet. When he saw Hannah, he crawled to her and held up his chubby arms. She lifted him, and he snuggled against her neck. Glancing at Peninnah, she noticed a strange expression on the second wife's face. Could it be compassion? Quickly the expression vanished, and Peninnah busied herself with adding wood to the cooking fire.

Throughout the day the women baked a good supply

of bread for the evening offering and for the journey home. Hannah bought pomegranates and dates from the vendors who wandered among the booths. Then she waited restlessly for sundown when she could return to the tabernacle for the evening worship. Smoke from the burning bullock still drifted down into the valley, reminding her of the sacrifice she was herself making. At last the sun sank behind the western trees, and to call the people for worship, Levites sang out their praise to the Lord.

Carrying fruit and bread, Elkanah and his family slowly ascended the stairway. *How tired I am,* Hannah realized. *Only the hope of seeing Samuel gives me strength to go on.* When they reached the tabernacle, she sighed. The singing Levites stood on the porch, and she tried to look behind them for a glimpse of her son. *Where is my boy in there?* she wondered.

When Eli's sons Hophni and Phinehas emerged, she stepped back. Strangely, instead of taking their usual places in the center of the porch, they stood to one side. The tabernacle doors opened again and Eli's large figure appeared through it. Behind him, a small boy wearing a brown and white robe dragged a big basket.

"There's Samuel," Othniel called out. "He's my brother."

The worshipers advanced to place their offerings at the feet of the priests. Some gave to Phinehas and Hophni, but most dropped their fruit and bread into the basket of the little boy in the brown and white robe. Soon tabernacle servants brought more containers and set them by Samuel. Othniel and the other brothers pushed through the crowd and with much giggling threw dates and pomegranates into his basket. He laughed with them.

Hannah and Elkanah made their way forward to stand in front of Samuel. When he saw them, he pointed to his basket and continued to smile.

Elkanah squeezed Hannah's hand. "Thanks to our God, Samuel is happy." He placed their offerings into the basket.

From behind Hannah, Peninnah's voice challenged, "Aren't you worried that Hophni and Phinehas will teach your son some of their greedy ways?"

"No," Hannah replied, "he has the right to find joy in the freewill offerings of the people. My son will not become greedy."

"How can you know that?"

"Because he's dedicated, and the Lord will protect him from any evil influence."

"Huh!" Peninnah sniffed. "You have a lot of faith."

Calmly, Hannah replied, "You need only to pray that the Lord will enter your heart, and you will have as much."

"Pray." Peninnah repeated the word as if it were foreign to her, and then in a softer tone it came again. "Pray."

At that moment Levite voices rang out in the evening worship adoration. "Praise to the Lord. Praise." The worshipers stepped away from the altar and the tabernacle porch to make room for the dancing maidens. A wistful smile played at Hannah's lips as she remembered the long-ago evening when Elkanah had watched her dance. She looked again toward the sanctuary. Now her tired little boy slumped down at the base of the same doorpost where she had petitioned the Lord to give her a son.

A tabernacle servant lifted Samuel and carried him into the sanctuary. Hannah yearned to follow, to see him safely onto his sheepskin and to tuck the blanket around him. Instead, with Elkanah by her side and Peninnah and her children trailing behind them, she slowly descended the stairway. Before she fell asleep in the booth, once again the comforting thought came: "I have fulfilled my promise to God."

Hannah awoke to the cool morning. The sun's rays were breaking across the eastern horizon, and already Nathan was bringing the donkeys for the women to load.

Peninnah lifted a bundle of sheepskins onto a donkey's back. "You're going to be lonesome," she remarked to Hannah.

"Of course I'll miss Samuel." Hannah piled blankets on top of the sheepskins and tied them securely with a flax rope. "But now that I've stopped nursing him, I'm sure I'll have more children."

"How can you be so sure?"

"I believe it's the Lord's will for me."

With the donkeys loaded, Elkanah led his family and servants westward. Part way up the winding mountain road they stopped to rest and eat their mid-morning meal of bread and figs. Hannah sat down next to her husband, and he accepted bread from her hand. Before he ate, he told her, "Yesterday I spoke to Eli about Samuel's schooling. He will teach him the duties of the tabernacle and also to read and write. With these skills and the high priest's influence, we can be sure he will give service to God."

A thoughtful expression crossed his face. "While I was speaking with Eli, Samuel came out of the tabernacle to stand in front of me. He was so excited, he shouted, 'Eli's going to teach me how to be a prophet. He's the high priest, and he knows how to show me.' Then Samuel threw his arms around my neck and said, 'He even says that God might talk to me.'"

Her husband's words sent a surge of hope rising in her breast. "Perhaps some day when he has grown to manhood, our son will return to Ramah and prophesy there."

"It could happen. We have been faithful to the Lord, and the Lord will be faithful to us."

The small caravan continued up the mountain trail to the patriarchal highway where Elkanah led the way southward until he reached the western road that wound its way to the valley floor and on to Ramah.

Peninnah and her children sank down onto an out-cropping of stone, but Hannah stood gazing to the north-east where she could see Shiloh faintly in the distance. The overcast sky and mist hovering in the valley ob-scured part of the view.

With a squirming baby in her arms, Peninnah glanced in the same direction. "Are you trying to see your son all the way from here?"

"No," Hannah answered calmly, "I'm thinking of how I will see him next harvest time when we travel to Shiloh. Each year I'll weave a little robe and take it to him when we go up for the sacrifice." She held out her arms to take the baby from his mother.

With a grateful sigh Peninnah handed her youngest son to Hannah.

Holding the child, Hannah turned away from the view to Shiloh and gazed far to the west toward Ramah, the place she had learned to love. A shaft of sunlight broke through the clouds and illuminated the road that led to the hill on which the town was built.

Her husband stood beside her, and she faced him. "We have always worshiped the Lord at Shiloh and that is good, but I'm sure He is with us at Ramah also."

"Yes," Elkanah agreed. "You have spoken well. God will watch over our son at the tabernacle and over us wherever we are." He took her hand and reached for Peninnah's to help her up from the rock. "Come, mothers of my children, let us journey on."

Epilogue

❦

"... and she (Hannah) conceived and bore three sons and two daughters" (1 Sam. 2:21, NKJV).

"And the child Samuel grew in stature and in favor both with the Lord and men" (verse 26, NKJV).

Also by Lois Erickson

Leah

"It is highly unlikely you will read this book and ever again see Jacob and his household as vague, dusty characters wandering about the book of Genesis," says fellow author June Strong. Here is the powerful, sympathetic story of Jacob's unwanted wife. Meet this Bible character who battled jealousy while striving for love and acceptance.
Paper, 138 pages. US$7.95, Cdn$11.55.

Huldah

From the moment she disguised herself to sneak him to the Temple, Huldah seemed destined to play a leading role in young Josiah's life. Through the Assyrian capture of King Manasseh and the evil reign and assassination of Prince Amon, she had risked all to secretly teach him the will of God. But now that Josiah was ready to begin his perilous work, could she trust God enough to let him go? Lois Erickson involves us in the intriguing story of a biblical prophet and reveals how her dauntless courage resulted in the reign of one of Israel's greatest kings.
Paper, 125 pages. US$7.95, Cdn$11.55.

Zipporah

She was a beautiful Midianite shepherd. He was an Egyptian prince fleeing for his life. She resisted the attraction between them as if she already knew what it would cost her to love one of the greatest men in Hebrew history. A fascinating portrayal of the lives of Zipporah and Moses.
Paper, 128 pages. US$7.95, Cdn.$11.55.